WITHDRAWN
FROM COLLECTION
VPL

# The Alchemist's Dream

# THE ALCHEMIST'S DREAM

Ψ

## JOHN WILSON

KEY PORTER BOOKS

Copyright © 2007 by John Wilson

All rights reserved. No part of this work covered by the copyrights hereon may
be reproduced or used in any form or by any means—graphic, electronic or mechani-
cal, including photocopying, recording, taping or information storage and retrieval
systems—without the prior written permission of the publisher, or, in case of photocopying or other reprographic copying, a licence from Access Copyright, the Cana-
dian Copyright Licensing Agency, One Yonge Street, Suite 1900, Toronto, Ontario,
M6B 3A9.

**Library and Archives Canada Cataloguing in Publication**

Wilson, John (John Alexander), 1951–
    The alchemist's dream / John Wilson.

ISBN-13: 978-1-55263-934-4, ISBN-10: 1-55263-934-7

1. Bylot, Robert—Juvenile fiction. 2. Hudson, Henry, d. 1611—Juvenile fiction.
3. Dee, John, 1527-1608—Juvenile fiction. 4. Northwest Passage—Discovery and
exploration—British—Juvenile fiction. I. Title.
PS8595.I5834A78 2007       jC813'.54       C2007-902112-3

THE CANADA COUNCIL | LE CONSEIL DES ARTS
FOR THE ARTS | DU CANADA
SINCE 1957 | DEPUIS 1957

ONTARIO ARTS COUNCIL
CONSEIL DES ARTS DE L'ONTARIO

The publisher gratefully acknowledges the support of the Canada Council for the
Arts and the Ontario Arts Council for its publishing program. We acknowledge the
support of the Government of Ontario through the Ontario Media Development
Corporation's Ontario Book Initiative.

We acknowledge the financial support of the Government of Canada through the
Book Publishing Industry Development Program (BPIDP) for our publishing activities.

Key Porter Books Limited
Six Adelaide Street East, Tenth Floor
Toronto, Ontario
Canada M5C 1H6

www.keyporter.com

Text design: Marijke Friesen
Electronic formatting: Shivani Vamra

Printed and bound in Canada

07 08 09 10 11 5 4 3 2 1

FOR SARAH, FIONA AND IAIN AS THEY
EMBARK ON THEIR VOYAGES OF DISCOVERY.

# Prologue

## The Alchemy of Age

Robert Bylot was waiting for death. He sat in a high-backed wooden chair, a threadbare blanket wrapped around his shoulders, staring into the dying embers of the fire that glowed in the stone hearth. His head was surrounded by unkempt white hair and a five-day growth of beard, and his wrinkled skin sagged as if his body were already beginning to decay. Discarded fragments of his supper lay in the folds of the blanket, and he was chewing thoughtfully on a branch of fennel to freshen his breath.

The modest room was one of two Bylot owned in the borough of Wapping, outside the ancient walls of London and across from the great shipyards of Deptford. It was not the residence of choice for those aspiring to social position; the streets were too narrow for a large carriage, and the characters who frequented the deep shadows of the overhanging buildings were not of the most genteel sort. The taverns supported the usual clientele of cutpurses and villains, but even the lowest often struck Bylot as no worse than many a crewman with whom he had sailed.

Bylot's apartment was located on the second floor above an apothecary shop, a location that kept him a little removed from the tumult and odour of the street. But the stairs were hard on his aged legs. The rooms were cramped and cluttered with the possessions of a busy life, but Bylot didn't mind. He had seen enough of empty space in his time.

Bylot's life had been long, eighty-five years as he had counted this past summer, and he was ready for it to end. But life clung to him like the wisps of white hair on his head, and each morning he awoke to the noises on the London street outside reminding him that he had to face another day.

It hadn't always been that way. As a boy, Bylot had dreamed of fame and glory—of sailing to the ends of the earth and seeing wondrous sights. And he had done it, too! But where had it all led? Everyone from his youth was dead and long forgotten by the world.

But Bylot remembered. The past lay in his mind—magical, glittering, and as real as the cold stone of the fireplace before him. And now, in the autumn of 1669, it was all that remained.

Surrounded by his possessions and his memories, Bylot sat, convinced that he still lived because his life was not yet complete. Something would happen to make sense of all the happiness and tragedy he had experienced; something to release him from the guilt he felt for what he had done a half-century before. He had no idea what this something was, but he waited, close by the Thames River that had launched so many of his dreams.

His answer came with a knock on his door.

Ψ

"Go away," Bylot mumbled. He had no desire to descend the stairs to the noisome street simply to face some drunken sailor who couldn't find his way home. But the knocking was repeated—urgent, insistent.

Grumbling, Bylot rose stiffly and descended. He pulled the door open and looked out on the cold night. Behind the hooded figure on his step, a fine, wetting rain made the cobbles glisten in the flickering lights from the windows across the way. In the background, the river softly slapped at its banks.

"Master Bylot?" the visitor asked.

"Aye," Bylot responded. "Who wishes to know?"

"Master Bylot, explorer, and lately mate on the bark Discovery?"

"Aye. Much lately I fear, but that is I." Bylot had not been called an explorer in many years, and mention of the Discovery brought memories flooding back.

"I bring a wondrous document from afar. Would you indulge my entry from this damnable night?" The voice was soft but clear. It suggested some intelligence, yet possessed an element of low cunning.

"Come in," Bylot said stepping aside. It was not his habit to allow strangers into his small home, especially mysterious ones in the dead of night, but the man's reference to the past intrigued him and he was beyond caring what evil might befall his frail body.

They climbed the creaking stairs in silent darkness. There, in the dim candlelight, the man removed his cloak and hood to reveal the rather shabby garb of a sailor. The clothes surprised Bylot. The tone of voice had led him to suspect the attire of a gentleman, or at least of a street charlatan. With a grunt, Bylot indicated the stool by the hearth and returned to his own chair.

When both were settled, Bylot examined his visitor. The man sitting across from him appeared close to thirty years of age. He had a clean-shaven, squarish, weather-beaten face topped by prematurely-thinning brown hair. His eyes were a watery blue and they regarded Bylot with an expression of smiling superiority. There was to his mouth an almost feminine cast, and his sharp tongue continually darted out to moisten the lips. In his right hand, the man carried a small bundle wrapped in oilcloth.

"What is your name and what do you want of me?" Bylot demanded.

"I am Robert Gilby," the man began, "newly returned from the northern wilderness of the Americas in the ketch *Nonsuch* under the Captaincy of Zachariah Gillam."

"I have heard of your voyage. In search of trade in furs to compete with the French, were you not?"

"Aye, and with some fair measure of attainment too."

"That is not what I heard. The word is that your sponsors will not retire on the proceeds of this voyage. How then, with no profit to show, can you count a commercial venture a success?"

"Our voyage proved what may be possible—but it is of little concern to me what befalls some company of adventurers. I simply voyaged as a diversion."

Bylot wondered how many that "diversion" had left in London, searching vainly for stolen purses or lost honour.

"I did my work," Gilby continued, "counted my pay as

profit, and saw something of that part of the world. In truth, I saw much of interest and not a little that leads me here tonight."

Gilby regarded his host shrewdly for a long moment. Bylot stared back, waiting.

"Since you have heard of our voyage, you will know well enough that we overwintered in the Great Sea called for Thomas Button, or sometimes for your first master, Henry Hudson?"

Bylot nodded.

"Well, 'tis a God-forsaken place and no mistake. We built a fort from the logs abundant there by a river we named Rupert on the shores of the bay named for old Captain James. We built in part upon the foundations of a rude dwelling said by some to have been constructed by Englishmen some sixty years previous. I think you know of this place?"

Bylot's mind flashed back to the winter of 1610. A ship lay, drawn up upon a barren shore, beside a rough-timbered house from which a thin stream of smoke escaped. Discarded equipment was strewn all around, poking blackly through the blanket of snow. Bent, ragged shapes went about a variety of tasks. A tall figure in a green, fur-collared coat stood some way off and gazed across the ice to the west.

"I might," Bylot said.

"Well," Gilby went on, "the season became wondrous cold, but we were well supplied and passed a snug enough time. Come spring the local savages came in to trade and we filled our holds with an abundance of excellent beaver pelts. The best kind we found were those already worn, for then the coarse hair was naturally eroded, leaving but the fine and saving one step for the hat maker. I fear there will be some savages who will feel the cold this winter for want of an extra layer of pelts."

"I am glad of your comfort and thank you for this lesson in the milliner's arts," Bylot said irritably, "but I do not see that it should be a concern of mine."

"Patience," the man continued through a lopsided smile that exposed several broken teeth. "All things come to those who wait.

"We traded with upward of ten score savages this spring past, but one old man, bent near double with the cares of a harsh life in the wilderness, caught my eye. He drew no attention to himself, yet he was in constant attendance upon our dealings. Near every day he could be found, watching, to one side, with no greater presence than a mote caught in the corner of one's eye. None of our doings escaped him, and yet he took no part nor seemed to wish for more than simply to observe. I began to watch him.

"At length, he became aware of my attention. Rather than being a discouragement, my notice seemed to please him and he attached himself to me where possible, always at a goodly distance but ever there. I neither threatened nor encouraged, preferring to wait and see what would happen.

"On the morning of the tide that was to bear us home, a large number of savages—men, women and children, both old and young—congregated in their primitive finery to bid us farewell and for one last chance to beg for trinkets and baubles. I was busy with the last of our preparations and was some little distance from my companions. All of a sudden, I was aware of the old man by my side, much closer than previous. I stopped and looked directly at him. He was swarthy as any savage and certainly the owner of their unpleasant odour. He was dressed in their habit of leggings and a loose shirt of animal hide, and wore a rough leather pouch hanging from a belt around his waist. His hair was grey and long and plastered down with some foul-smelling animal fat."

Gilby paused.

"What did he want?" Bylot asked, impatiently.

"I see you now wish to hear my tale," Gilby sneered. "You shall, and then we will see about some business.

"The old man was as close as I am to you. I would have been loathe to allow this, but I had taken an interest in him, so I stood my ground and waited. I have seen many wonders in my travels, but what transpired next surprised even me. Instead of the begging hand or the offered worthless tool, the old man spoke, and not the singsong gibberish of his people, but the King's English."

Gilby paused again. Bylot's mind was a restless turmoil of possibilities.

"For God's sake," he shouted. "What did he say?"

Gilby smiled. "It was not easy to understand his speech. At first, I did not even recognize it as my own language, so rough and arcane was its mode. But with repetition, I began to make something out of it. The first thing he said was, 'Did any live?'"

"And what did he mean by that?" Bylot interrupted.

"I know not. I asked, but got no response other than repetition of the phrase wrapped in local dialect. I fear that life in the wilds had unhinged his mind."

"Was anything else he said intelligible?"

"Little that I could make out with certainty. There were a few words and phrases I could understand with effort; 'Desire Provoketh,' 'God's Mercy' and 'Michaelmass' were most often repeated, but meant nothing to me. There were also sounds that might have been attempts at our speech. I suspected I heard 'discovery' at one place in his discourse, but it was not repeated. The old man seemed particularly keen that I learn his name even though it meant as little to me as the others I had heard. The savages thereabouts place much stock in names and exchange them freely amongst each other and with strangers."

"What was his name?"

"As close as I could make out, and transposed into the spelling we found most useful for recording the utterances of the savages for trade, it was Dja-khu-tsan."

"And he uttered nothing else?"

"Nothing but repetition of what I have told you.

"Now that I was over my surprise at his first words, I saw he was only an old, mind-weakened savage. Truly, he must have had some contact with an English party and had picked up a few words with which he was trying to impress me. But it was also obvious that I could learn naught of import from him.

"I turned to go, as we were near to departing. As I did so, the old man reached forward and grabbed my arm. His grip was surprisingly strong, and I was annoyed at him laying on a hand. I turned back and raised my free hand to strike him away. But my blow never fell. Certainly the man cowered away in fear, but he did not loose his grip and his other hand offered me a book." Gilby held out the package he had been holding by his side. "*This* book."

Bylot reached over to take it, but it was drawn back.

"Not yet," Gilby said. "This is the hub of the business I would conduct with you—by which we shall both profit—and I would finish my tale."

Bylot clenched his outstretched hand in frustration.

"Well," Gilby slowly set the book on his knee and locked his fingers together below his chin. "I at once realized the possible import of what the old man held. It was not of savage generation, they having no writing to speak of. Therefore it must have come to this place through abandonment or loss by some explorer. As I knew, the unfortunate Master Hudson had disappeared mysteriously hereabouts greater than fifty years previously. Perhaps this document, so strangely offered to me in the wilderness, held some answers that I might profit from.

"Not wishing to weaken my bargaining position, I retained a stern appearance and spoke harshly to the effect that he should unhand me forthwith. To my surprise he did so and, to my even greater surprise, made no attempt to bargain. He placed the book in my hand, turned away, and shuffled off into the trees. I hid the book from sight and made way back to my companions.

"I was, I frankly admit, excited by this odd turn of events, yet, with the bustle of setting sail and the cramped confines of our quarters, we were several days at sea before I found the opportunity to examine my new possession in privacy."

Bylot's mind was racing. "Desire Provoketh," "God's Mercy" and "Michaelmass" were all names he remembered only too well. They were names given by Henry Hudson to geographical features he'd discovered all those years ago. And *Discovery* was the name of Hudson's ship. The savage could have come by this knowledge only from contact with one of Hudson's crew. And the book—Bylot had not seen it, yet he was certain what it was. It was his past come back to haunt him. A deep past, like a ruined city of the ancients, buried and forgotten in sand until its streets and walls are uncovered by wind.

"I'm not well versed in the art of reading," Gilby continued. "I can decipher a broadsheet or the Lord Mayor's proclamation well enough—better than some I daresay—and in my line of work that has always more than sufficed." Gilby licked his lips and leered at Bylot. "After all, my usual acquaintances are more familiar with the card and blade than Master Shakespeare's tragedies.

"Nonetheless, upon examining the old native's book, I immediately apprehended its import. It has been much ill used by time and fate, not being placed with its companions in some learned man's library press. Still and all, it is of some value.

"Upon my return, I planned to seek out some antiquarian of wealth who might be prepared to part with a few crowns for the privilege of examining these pages. However, chance placed me one night in the company of some friends in the Pie Tavern, but a short distance from here toward the city. I was, I admit, the worse for too much ale and porter and was elaborating upon my late voyage to all who would listen. I of course did not mention my find, but one old patron listened with uncommon attention. As I finished my tale, he approached and engaged me in conversation. It seems you frequent that establishment from time to time and are in the habit of confiding your adventures to this very same person. Thus it was that I learned of your continued tenure on this Earth and conceived the idea of our current business. You are not an easy man to find, Master Bylot, but, as you see, I have sought you out."

"What is the book?" Bylot asked with scarcely controlled impatience.

"Oh!" said Gilby with feigned surprise, "have I not mentioned that? How remiss. Here, read for yourself." He unwrapped the book and held it out. Bylot fixed his glasses on his nose and leaned forward. His heart beat dangerously fast in his old chest.

The book was a small, octavo volume, bound in dark leather and held closed by a brass clasp. The cover was heavily stained.

Bylot breathed deeply and ran his gnarled fingers over the rich tangle of words scrawled in a familiar curling script on its cover.

*This be the Sole and Onlie Jornall and Testament e of Mayster Henrie Hudson, Maryner and Explorer in the Wyldernefs.*

"I see from your expression that I have come to the right person," Gilby went on, his sharp tongue darting out to moisten his lips. "Surely this volume must be worth a few guineas. They will not mean much to such as you but will greatly ease the lot of a poor sailor like myself. Shall we say five guineas?"

It was outrageous, but Bylot was too weak to argue. Rising and shuffling dazedly to the other room he retrieved his purse, extracted the required sum, and returned. Bylot flung the money onto the other man's lap. "You are a thief and a villain, Gilby, and you deserve not one farthing of this money. Yet I will pay it, if only to see the memory of brave men preserved."

Gilby laughed and placed the book in Bylot's shaking hands. "Aye, if you wish. I care not what you do with these old scratched words."

"Our business is done, be gone. You have caused enough upset to memory for one night."

Gilby collected the coins, stood and retrieved his cloak. "I thank you, Master Bylot, and I shall toast your health before long."

Then he was gone. A quick blast of cold air from the street door and Bylot was alone, his mind a turmoil of memory.

He gazed at the book on his lap. It had been a lifetime since he had held it last. He knew some of what it contained—but what had been added? What had been written by a starving man huddled hopelessly on a barren shore, waiting for rescue that never came—was it Bylot's release from guilt, or a final condemnation? Desire and fear wrestled in the old man's mind. He ran his fingers over the volume's brass clasp. So easy to open and read, but easier, perhaps, to leave closed. After all, death would provide its own answers.

Ψ

A screamed curse and a snatch of an old sea song from the raucous alley below brought a shouted "No!" from Bylot's lips. The goings-on outside meant nothing to him, but they provoked a reaction nonetheless.

With much effort, Bylot placed the book on his table, slid from his chair and adjusted his blanket round his shoulders. Painfully, he crouched on the hearth and wrapped his arthritic fingers around a fresh log. From the pile of embers, small flames licked eagerly at the dry wood, casting light on the old man's face and briefly banishing the shadows. Bylot stood and rested an arm on the mantle—allowing the warmth to rejuvenate him. He looked around as if seeing the room for the first time.

"What is real?" he croaked. "My few possessions, my memories, the life beyond my window, the ghosts that haunt me—the book?"

Bylot pulled the blanket tighter and let his gaze shift to the mantle and slide along the array of oddly shaped, coloured glass bottles resting there.

"Once in the northern regions," he told the bottles, "I saw a city hanging in the air beneath a waving curtain of green light bright enough to read my compass by. Towers, battlements and minarets were so clearly defined that I was convinced of their reality, but as I sailed on, the city wavered, became transparent and vanished to be replaced by a blank, ice-reflecting sky. Our weak senses are often confused."

Bylot reached over and picked up a curious-looking globe. It was compact enough to fit in the palm of his hand, yet it housed other globes. Its surface was covered with wonderfully detailed etchings—designs that Bylot's old eyes could barely make out. Within, powders lay and pale liquids swirled in their separate compartments.

Bylot held the delicate glass before him, turning it slowly as he gazed into its depths. "I hold the universe in my hand," he said, recalling lessons learned many years before. "Fire, Earth, Water, Air, Aqua fortis and Aqua vitae. Should I crush these fragile spheres, the powers unleashed would end my doubts."

Bylot smiled ruefully. "Like the dreams of Doctor Dee and the Alchemists, you are nothing now. The world has left you and me behind. All that is left are my memories. Within my mind, Dee still lives—talking with angels and struggling to turn lead into gold. Henry Hudson still sails the unknown seas, searching for his impossible path to Cathay. Henry Greene and Robert Smythe still play their games. And I still stand amid them all. Only I remember what Dee sought, why Hudson failed and how Greene and Smythe played for profit. But even I don't know it all."

Bylot returned the globe to its resting place, shuffled back to his chair and picked up the book. Gently, he caressed the cover. "I dread the words you might hold, and yet they are the only path to my salvation. Only in these pages can I be forgiven. Only you can end my story. But to end, I must first begin."

# I

## Childhood

Robert Bylot's earliest memories were of loneliness. It could not all have been like that—he knew there were wonderful times with his sister, Evelyn—but it was the solitary moments in the dark corners of the rambling house at Hoddesdon, a day's journey outside London, that stuck in his mind.

His favourite corner was a tiny brick space hidden behind the produce barrels in the pantry. At some time in the past, it had been an angle in the outside wall of the house, but an extension had been added as the family prospered. To even the lie of the walls, this small space had been declared unusable and bricked in. But the old bricks had been poorly cemented and the inquisitive Bylot had one day discovered that enough could be removed to allow entry. The space within was only two feet in width by four long, yet it stretched up the full three floors of the house. There was barely enough room for a small boy to squeeze into, but he was not a large child and it was adequate enough to be his refuge from the worries of the world—his bolt hole.

The space had a small opening to the outside world near the top that allowed some fresh air to enter and provided the merest flicker of light on bright days. Unfortunately, it also allowed the entry of numerous small insects and creatures, which often fell on Bylot as he sat. These occasionally caused some discomfort but he grew accustomed to the spiders and assorted tiny creatures who shared his hiding place.

On one occasion, Bylot was sitting deep in thought when he heard a rustling above. It sounded like a creature much larger than the usual, and his six-year-old heart began to race. He could have crawled out and escaped, but fear froze him in place. The noise came steadily closer as dislodged pieces of dirt and brick fell about him. Bylot crunched himself into as small a space as possible, closed his eyes and prayed for the intruder to go away.

The noise seemed deafening in the confined space and time slowed unbearably. Eventually, Bylot felt it—soft, feathery tendrils rapidly brushing his face and sharp claws scratching his cheek. Wildly, he lashed out. His hand connected with something in the darkness and crushed it with panicked violence against the wall. Silence descended.

After a long time, Bylot's heart returned to normal and his mind regathered its perspective. Feeling around on the floor, he discovered the still-warm body of a starling. Having entered at the top of the hide, the bird had become disoriented and flown down seeking escape. Bylot's childish mind had imagined all kinds of horrors in the unknown, and in his fear he had struck out unthinkingly and killed the poor beast.

Guilt at the unnecessary death soon replaced Bylot's fear, and he carefully took the tiny body to show it to Evelyn. She was a year older than him and would know what to do to make things right.

"We must bury it," she said, seriously.

Together the pair made a small wooden box, carried the coffin out into the woods and buried it with exaggerated care and many tears beneath an ancient oak tree.

"You have nothing to feel guilt over," Evelyn explained as they walked back to the house.

"But I killed one of God's innocent creatures," Bylot said.

"Yes, but consider, God created the circumstances of your act. He created your terror."

"And I prayed to him for it to stop," Bylot said fervently.

"It's a natural human reaction, established by God, to react sometimes with violence when faced with fear. Is it reasonable of God to expect a small child to overcome this?"

"I don't know." Bylot was confused. Was it right to question God? Could God make a mistake? What about the guilt? If his fear came from God, didn't his guilt as well? And although the fear had long gone, the guilt was still there, despite Evelyn's comforting words.

Ψ

Six years later, Bylot sat cross-legged before the intricately carved wood of the fireplace in the great hall, his hand delicately tracing the riotous ornamentation of leaves, vines and fruits that the master carver had created. It was a lost world that hid all manner of extraordinary beasts and men. Bylot felt that, if he could only stare hard enough, the vines would part and he would be rewarded with a glimpse of this unknown, magical place—a place where monsters, mermen and dragons dwelled, where savages with faces upon their chests and no heads cavorted in lands where trees grew downward and rain, hail and snow fell upward.

Bylot knew these marvels existed because he had read the reports and seen the maps of travellers who had ventured to the ends of the earth. The tales they brought back, which Bylot found in the books at his local grammar school, fuelled his imagination. As he read and learned, he craved seeing these things for himself. Over the years, the desire became an obsession. Bylot spent long hours alone, hunched over a flickering candle, copying pieces of maps and pages of text. These he brought home to show Evelyn, who, being a girl, was not allowed to attend school. Then he hid them in his bolt hole. His childhood refuge was too small for him to fit in now, but it was perfect for storage. Bylot thought of it as his secret library; secret because his father—a domineering, distant, practical man—strongly disapproved of what he considered a frivolous interest in exploration.

But to Bylot, exploration was anything but frivolous. Francis Drake, Martin Frobisher and John Davis were his heroes, the voyagers who led the way into a bright new future where all things were possible. And one day, Bylot knew, despite his father, *he* would join their ranks. He would go to these far places and see these things for himself. He would become a famous explorer, tame geography and chart the courses of unknown rivers and the intricacies of mysterious coastlines. He would create the most wonderful map of the world ever seen.

"Robert, look what I've found." Evelyn bounded across the polished oak floor and skidded to a halt beside her brother. Despite being older, she looked up to him because he attended school while she could not. Both thought this horribly un-fair. Evelyn possessed an insatiable curiosity about the natural world and was being denied the chance to learn about it. Since she had been old enough to walk, Evelyn had collected and studied the creatures she found in the local ponds or beneath the hedgerows, or curiosities she dug out of the soft white chalk in the hills round Hoddesdon. She craved learning and often brought her discoveries to her younger brother for identification. For his part, Bylot copied whatever he could of the books at school and brought the pages back for Evelyn to digest.

"I found it up on the hill. It took me all morning to scratch it out of the white stone. What do you think it is?" Evelyn's grey eyes shone with enthusiasm and her cheeks glowed with the effort of running back with her prize.

"It's a Horn of Ammon," Bylot replied, taking the small, tightly curled object from her. "I think it's the shell of a sea creature."

Evelyn's brow furrowed. "How could a sea creature find its way into the rock on top of a hill?"

"Learned men suppose that either these long-dead crea-tures are carved in place within the rock as sports of nature, or that they are evidence of Noah's Deluge and were depos-ited on hilltops by the floodwaters."

"That's nonsense." Evelyn spoke so loudly that Bylot glanced around the hall.

"And that's blasphemy. Don't let the minister hear you say that."

"But it can't be true," Evelyn persisted. "How can shells as exquisite and detailed as these be carved within solid rock? And would not the force of a torrent created by rain have been from the hills, along the rivers, and to the sea rather than lifting sea life from the sea and placing it atop hills? It does not make sense."

"How then do you explain its presence?"

Evelyn's face fell. "I don't know. But there must be another answer."

Bylot laughed. "That's what you always say. Why can't you just accept what the philosophers tell us?"

"Because they are wrong."

"And you will find the correct answers?"

"Perhaps," Evelyn said defensively. "And I would find the answers faster if I were allowed to attend school and learn."

"I tell you everything I learn."

"I know. I shouldn't complain. I am lucky to have a little brother who thinks I am important enough to teach! But it is you who will leave and go off to all these wonderful, exotic places you tell me about."

"And I shall sail through the Straits of Anian, capture a proud Spanish galleon, visit the Spice Islands and sail back to shower you with jewels and cloves. I shall dedicate the book of my adventures to you."

"I am honoured," Evelyn gave an exaggerated bow, "but it's not the same as going. And where are the Straits of Anian, anyway?"

"It is what the Spanish call the passage from the Atlantic to the Pacific Ocean, around the top of the Americas. It is said it must exist to balance the route that Ferdinand Magellan discovered to the south. John Davis and Francis Drake both searched unsuccessfully for it, but I shall find it."

"If father permits you."

At the mention of his father, the enthusiasm drained from Bylot. "I won't let him stop me."

"Robert, why do you hate him so? A son should get on with his father."

"I don't hate him, Evelyn."

"What then?"

For an age, Bylot was silent. "Telling you won't repair anything," he said at last. "It will simply change the way you see him."

Now it was Evelyn's turn to look pensive. "I see him more clearly than you think. He is distant and disapproves of your interest in the sea, but he rules me with a much harder hand. I am not allowed to attend school, but there is nothing to prevent a tutor being hired. I have asked—no, I have *begged* him to do that—but he always says no. He tells me it is not a woman's place to learn, that knowledge will merely spoil me as a good and loyal wife.

"You will leave here eventually, Robert, and then you may do as you wish. For me there is no escape. Already Father is talking of which local son will make a suitable match. We have argued and fought over this, but he is adamant and I can see no way out. It is just the way he believes the world should be. But what has he ever done to you?"

"Very well. I will tell you." Bylot sighed. "But you must swear never to tell a living soul."

"I swear."

"I do not hate him, I fear him. Once, the summer I turned eight years old, I tried to talk to Father as he sat in the herb garden. I wanted to know about Mother. I know she died before I can remember and that I resemble her very closely, but she is never talked of. I wanted to learn of her and I reasoned that Father, sitting as he was, content among the pleasant odours of fennel, rosemary and sage, would be willing to talk.

"I came up quietly and seated myself in the dust of the path at his feet. He ignored me.

"'Father,' I began tentatively. ''Tis a fine summer's eve and the garden is in splendid order.' Father merely grunted in response.

"'My favourite is the mint. I find the smell pleasing.' I rambled on but with no greater response. I decided my only recourse was to come straight to the point.

"'I was wondering.' I said, 'was mother fond of the garden, too?'

"Father ceased his gazing and fixed his eyes on me as if noticing me for the first time. It took a lot of courage, but I continued.

"'Father, I wish to know more of my mother. I know nothing of her. She is never talked of and yet I am told that I resemble her much. Will you not share some memories with me? I would much like...' I stopped. Father's eyes were filling with tears. Pity overwhelmed me and, instinctively, I reached out to touch him in comfort.

"At my movement, Father's expression, which had been growing ever more wistful, hardened into something, I was horrified to see, approaching hatred. Then he kicked me. I didn't have a chance to move—he just lashed out with his left foot. It caught me a heavy blow under the ribs, cracking one, I think, from the length of time it took for the pain to go, and making me gasp and fall back.

"I was winded and helpless as he stood up. I thought he was going to hit me again, but he simply said, 'Never, never, let me discover thee speaking of thy mother more.' Then he turned and stumbled back into the house."

Robert fell silent as Evelyn placed her arm around his shoulders.

"I was terrified," Bylot went on, close to tears. "For many months, my heart raced every time I was near him, fearing that he would lash out again without reason. But I was mystified, too. He had hit me before, but always in response to some fault of mine. I might question the degree of punishment, but always there was some punishment due. This time, I could see nothing that I had done wrong. I was expressing a natural curiosity and was punished harshly for it."

Evelyn squeezed her brother's shoulders. "Father loved Mother more than anything else in the world. Her death was a frightful blow to him."

"I know, just as it would be a frightful blow to me if anything happened to you, but why take it out on me?"

"I think because you look so much like her. It must be a continual reminder of what he has lost."

"You always think the best of everyone, Evelyn. It is not my fault I resemble her."

"I know, but there is something else. Do you know when Mother died?"

"When I was very young."

"Our mother died as you were being born."

Ψ

Over the years, each of Bylot's attempts at closeness with his father failed, but the violence of that afternoon in the herb garden was never repeated. Instead, his father became even more distant and days would sometimes go by without the pair setting eyes on each other. Bylot's loneliness increased, especially as his and Evelyn's path's diverged.

Although brother and sister still confided their hopes and fears to each other, Bylot was scheduled to go to Cambridge to study logic, rhetoric and arithmetic. Evelyn, on the other hand, was being groomed to marry a neighbouring landowner's son—David Aubrey, a dull youth whom she accurately mimicked mercilessly, to Bylot's huge amusement. Neither course was destined to bring joy, but each appeared unchangeable.

In the spring of 1599, as Bylot was turning fifteen, his father took sick. He had been in only middling health all winter, prone to attacks of coughing and more than once taking to his bed with the chills. One Sunday Bylot went to seek him out with a view to discussing his further educational prospects.

He found him standing in the hallway, as was becoming more common those days, facing a tapestry of the Prodigal Son. The tapestry showed the son returning, dishevelled and defeated, after deserting his family to seek his fortune. Bylot had always thought it odd how the father in the picture wore such a ridiculous expression of pleasure at his wayward son's return to the fold. He had never seen his own father look like that.

His father's back was towards Bylot and, as the boy approached, it was convulsed by a fit of coughing. Bylot placed a comforting hand on his father's shoulder. The old man jerked backward and spun to stare at his son. The sight shocked Bylot. His father's face was haggard from the effort of his cough, and he held a kerchief to his chin. The kerchief was stained with blood and a thin line of the same ran from the corner of his slack mouth.

"Father!" Bylot exclaimed. "What is wrong?"

"Be certain, lad, that thou doth naught to offend thy father," the old man croaked, "and if thou dost, be equal sure that thou doth make thy peace while there be still time. You are but . . ." His father's tirade was cut off by another fit of coughing. Placing his arm around him, Bylot half led, half carried the sick man to his room and laid him among his carved posts and heavy drapes.

Bylot summoned the physician—a worthy man much acquainted with the benefits of a wide range of herbs—who bled and purged his father and prescribed several potions and an abstinence of strong wine. For a time, the regime appeared to have a beneficial effect and the household looked to a recovery, but it was merely the first of many false hopes.

Throughout that summer, Bylot's father swung between the extremes of near death and apparent recovery, each time left weaker and less able to withstand the next onslaught. Many nights Bylot and Evelyn sat with him as he drifted in and out of uneasy slumber. Despite the harsh way Bylot had been treated over the years, he was concerned for his father's well-being. If the old man recovered because of Bylot's care, he might forgive and the pair could begin a normal father-son relationship. It was not to be.

By late September, everyone was exhausted and the house in turmoil. Bylot had not slept a full night in weeks, and Evelyn and the servants drifted about hollow-eyed and gaunt as ghosts. His father barely had the strength to stand by his bed for a moment or two, and was convulsed with fits of vomiting blood and bile almost daily.

Bylot found himself wishing for an end to his father's suffering, but the sick man hung on and all Bylot got for his prayers was guilt at wishing his father dead.

On the final night, Evelyn had gone to her room for rest and Bylot had fallen into a doze by the sickbed. His confused dreams often took him to the tapestry of the Prodigal Son. The images disturbed him greatly, yet upon awakening, he never could discern why that particular Bible story should have a special relevance. After all, he was no Prodigal Son. True, he wished to pursue a dream that his father didn't approve of, but much of his preparation for that had been in secret. As far as his father knew, Bylot was headed for Cambridge and a life in the city.

Bylot was awakened by the pressure of his father's bony fingers on his arm. He jerked his head up, unsure whether he was awake or dreaming, to see his father looking at him. His deep eyes burned with the unnatural glow of fever and he stared at his son's face intently. The pair remained that way for a long moment, Bylot silent and withstanding the glare, and then his father spoke in a voice stronger than any he had been capable of for weeks.

"Mine own father forgave me not," he said. "His desire was for a sailor son to fulfill his own unrequited dreams. He loved the sea with passion. I did not. The emptiness of it terrified me. I could be no Hawkins, as he wished. I could not satisfy him and so I learned to hate."

Bylot's father coughed once before continuing. "He died ere I could repent my hate and beg forgiveness for the unfulfilled expectations of my life."

The memory of his father's words in front of the tapestry flooded back. "Father, I do not hate you ...," he began, his thoughts stumbling out in confusion. But his father stopped him, tightening his grip on Bylot's arm.

"Fool! Ye understand nothing," he said. "'Tis not thou who hates, it is I. I hate thee."

Even though it explained much about his father's attitude over the years, the words stunned Bylot. "For what?" he stammered.

A bitter smile flickered over his father's thin lips. "For Jane," he said. "In death she gave thee life, yet she was my life. She saved me from mine own father and gave me the vigour to crawl from beneath his shadow. Ye took that life away.

"From the moment of thy first breath and her last, I have hated thee with a terrible passion. Oh, I hid it, but not a moment has gone by in thy presence when I have not cursed thy very existence. And what is worse, it is still there. Even now, facing death and an eternity of the torments of Hell, I cannot find it within my soul to forgive thee—mine own son. I am damned, so damn thee, too, Robert Bylot."

Exhausted from the effort, the old man collapsed back upon his pillows, breathing shallowly. Bylot sat in horror, overwhelmed by guilt. His father was right to hate him for killing the woman he loved. Bylot strongly resembled his mother. Every moment of his life must have been a torture for his father, a blade stabbing through the old man's heart every time he laid eyes upon the familiar face.

Bylot's father spoke no more. He did not need to. Every one of his final words had cut through his son like a red-hot poker. As the birds took up their morning song, the old man simply ceased to be. Bylot knew the instant of it, though he was at the time as lost in his own pitying thoughts as he had been the entire night. He looked up from his lap where his eyes had been resting in shame. His father was gone. All that remained was an empty shell, eyes staring upward at nothing, soul fled to whatever awaited it. This, Bylot realized, was the moment he had been waiting for. Not just that night, but from the very moment awareness of the world about him had entered his brain. He was free.

With eyes charged with tears, Bylot stood. He reached over and, in a final gesture of filial care, closed his father's eyes. Then he turned and walked out.

In the hall he met Evelyn, sleep still heavy on her eyes.

"He's dead."

Evelyn sighed and nodded. "It is for the best. I doubt I could have borne seeing him suffer much longer. I will go and see him and then we must arrange the funeral. There is much to do."

"I will not be here to help. I closed his eyes in death; that was my final duty. I am leaving this morning for London."

Evelyn nodded. "Then I wish you luck."

"And I you."

The pair embraced and, as the sun rose on his left, Bylot walked toward London.

# 2

# LONDON

As the sun rose higher and the clouds of dust thrown up by weary feet and passing carriages thickened, Bylot trudged south. He had no clear idea of what lay ahead, only of what was behind. He walked with his head down, ignoring the other travellers and the villages he passed through. Around mid-morning, he stopped at an inn and spent a few of his precious pennies on some bread and soup. He talked to no one and, as soon as his bowl was clean, set out once more. His feet hurt and his muscles ached, but he never once regretted his action. London, and his dreams of the sea and glory, pulled him on.

At length, in the early afternoon, Bylot crested a final ridge in the chalk downs and saw the metropolis laid out before him—a sea of blackened rooftops and smoking chimneys, pierced by sharp church spires. A shiver of disquiet passed through him. Bylot had heard from passing travellers and preaching churchmen that the city before him was an unrivalled concentration of vice and evil, waiting to draw in the naive and unwary to a life of corruption and debauchery. Was that what awaited him?

But as he stared, Bylot began to see London differently. The history he had been taught at school flooded over him. The city was simply the most recent expression of this place; layers of the past were buried beneath. The villages of Bylot's Saxon ancestors, the longhouses of the Danes, the forts and temples of the Romans, the rude huts of the barbarians—they all formed a vertical tapestry stretching far back to the time when monsters walked the land and left their bones in the clay.

Bylot was so aware of the past as he approached the city walls that had a toga-clad Roman senator or rude Saxon carl come forth from the gate to greet him he would not have been surprised. As it was neither did; only the distinctive odour of the streets wafted out to greet his arrival.

The smell that met him at the gates nearly rendered him unconscious. Being from the country, he was familiar with the odours of both human and animal natural functions, but the smell rising from the open sewers in the streets of London was like a physical thing assaulting him. He recognized many of the robuster fragrances—rotting vegetation, sweat and excrement—but some sickly sweet ones he did not, and their imagined origins made him hurry on his way and keep his mouth firmly shut.

Street artists of all kinds—jugglers, hawkers and organ grinders—thronged the way, jostling and shouting to attract attention. Washerwomen shouted their conversations and others, with brightly lipsticked faces, beckoned him into dark corners. Figures, both male and female, lay drunk in the filth, oblivious to the world about them. As Bylot moved through the narrow, crowded thoroughfares of the city, he was struck most strongly by the vibrant chaos around him. It seemed as if all aspects of life were being conducted, without pattern, as hurriedly as possible, on the open street. He was amazed, yet he struggled not to show it, desperate not to appear like the country bumpkin that he was.

Bylot had no clear destination in mind when he entered the city. Even if he had, he was so rapidly absolutely lost that it would have meant nothing. Eventually, he found himself in the neighbourhood of St. Paul's great church. For an age in the late daylight, he stood in awe of the buttressed walls, soaring, as it seemed, to the very heavens.

Bylot remembered how he and Evelyn had sat over etchings of the great church, wondering what it would be like to see it. A pang of loneliness stabbed at his chest. He wished Evelyn could see this place too. One day, he promised himself, when he was established, he would bring his sister here to see this wonder.

Bylot approached the west doors. He looked up at the carvings around the archway and was suddenly struck by the thought that this was where he was meant to be. Saints, sinners, the damned, the elect, devils and all manner of birds and beasts flocked in tumult around the throne of the Christ, and all were entwined in a jungle of magnificent foliage. Was this not the way into the fireplace carvings of his childhood? Through this magnificent door, perhaps, lay the key to his dreams.

Inside, the church was almost as busy with noise and movement as the street. Children ran about, beggars solicited alms, merchants sold all manner of salves and charms and, from many dozens of alters, the voices of chantry priests rose in supplication for deceased benefactors. The wide aisles of the church provided a shortcut for Londoners too busy, lazy or weary to go around the great building, and a priest was stationed at the door to prevent the entry of those with horses or mules. From the crypt beneath echoed the clack of printing presses busily manufacturing broadsheets and pamphlets for the edification of the populace.

Behind the alter screen, mysteries were being performed and the smell of incense filled Bylot's nostrils—a pleasant enough change from the odours of the street. But the building's majesty overcame all the petty, human activity. The instant he entered, Bylot's eyes were drawn, as the builders had intended, upward to the vault of heaven. Impossibly high above—surmounting bright portrayals of the lives of the saints and illustrative scenes from the gospels, between brightly painted pillars and a roof that held, against an unbelievably blue background, the stars of the sky—the magnificent windows shone with glory. The light—blue, red and gold—must surely be directly from God.

The greatest window of all was above the door Bylot had entered. The wall that had appeared so solid from the outside was, from within, a riot of light, held together only by the inspired will of its creator. A vast rose of coloured scenes of secular and spiritual life let in the rays of the setting sun in shafts of colour that surrounded Bylot in glory. It was all he could do to stop himself falling to his knees in fervent prayer. He had not felt the power of religion this strongly since he had been a small child, kneeling in the village church at Hoddesdon, surrounded by praying adults.

That he did not fall to his knees was due mostly to the jostling mass of people who continued to stream through the building. Bylot let himself be swept by them, all the while gazing upward like an idiot. At length he found himself before the tomb of some great lord and his lady. He lowered his head and regarded the scene.

The couple lay in stone, arrayed in their finery. Everything from the delicate ruffs at their necks to the laces on their shoes was carved in precise detail. Their faces looked as if only a little warmth would open the eyes and bring a smile to living lips. A small dog lay asleep at their feet.

Beneath was a different story. There, the couple lay again, but this time as the Last Judgment would find them. With as much care as with the sleeping pair, the carver had represented them as transi, half-decomposed corpses. The finery was rags and only shreds of their well-fed flesh clung to shining bones. Maggots swarmed in blank eye sockets and gaping skulls grinned. Even the skeleton of the dog was there. On a stone scroll at the couple's heads, were carved the words, "As ye are now, so once were we. As we are now, so ye shall be."

As Bylot examined the scene with morbid fascination, a voice behind him spoke.

"Cheerful, are they not?" The voice was smooth, with a hint of a west country accent.

Bylot turned to see a youth about the same age as himself. The young man was taller by a full three inches, but he was skinny and his long arms and legs stuck out from his body, making him appear almost spider-like. His face was narrow, his nose and chin sharp, and he sported the first wisps of a thin beard. His eyes were a peculiar greenish-grey and seemed, by a trick of the coloured rays from the great rose window, to have an internal light of their own.

He was well dressed in a woollen jerkin and leggings, and sported leather boots of such a quality and cleanliness that they made Bylot stare. The newcomer looked down at his own feet and laughed. "'Tis low work, but a cobbler never starves. You're new to the city?"

"I am," Bylot replied. "How do you know?"

The thin youth laughed loudly. "From your gawky look. Nobody but a newcomer does anything but hurry through or conduct business within these walls. Where are you from?"

"Hoddesdon," Bylot said. "I am on my way to seek seaborne employment."

"A sailor boy, no less. Then we are well met indeed. My name is Henry Greene, late of Limehouse but now seeking my fortune in the city proper. Like you, I am of a mind to take to the foam."

Greene bowed with an exaggerated flourish and rose smiling.

"My name is Robert Bylot. I have little experience of city ways, but I am strong and willing to learn, and aim to one day make a mark upon the world."

"Well said." Greene held out his hand. "I am pleased to be your friend, Robert Bylot. Mayhap we shall make a mark together. But for now, I know of a place where, this very evening, you might profit in your ambition, if you will let me be of service."

Bylot nodded agreement. Greene took his hand and shook it firmly. "Well then," he continued, "perhaps you will follow me."

Greene turned and worked his way back out of the church. Bylot hesitated, assailed suddenly by doubt. He knew nothing about this confident stranger. What if this was the way one was led into vice and debauchery? But what choice did he have? Where else could he go? And he had to decide soon—already Greene was becoming hard to see through the crowd. Bylot moved forward. He would take his chances.

The pair soon pushed their way out of the bustle around the church and entered the quieter streets of the business district. In the twilight, Bylot peered into the carriage arches leading into the courtyards of the guilds along the way. Each had elaborate coats of arms above grandiose names. Bylot's favourite was the drapers, or, as they wished to be known, the Master and Wardens and Brethren and Sisters of the Guild or Fraternity of the Blessed Mary the Virgin of the Mystery of Drapers of the City of London. Their crest was magnificent—a blazon of three sunbeams issuing from three flaming clouds surmounted by three Imperial crowns of gold on a shield of brightest azure. The blazon was supported by two grand lions and topped by a helm and crest with a golden ram upon it.

"It's just a group of cloth merchants," Greene said when he noticed Bylot hesitate. "We are headed for much grander prospects."

At length the pair reached Founders Hall, a large, two-storey, richly-carved square building. Light poured from the row of tall, mullioned windows, and the babble of many voices spilled out of the arched doorway. Inside, the main hall was panelled in dark wood and the ceiling heavily beamed. At the far end a fireplace that dwarfed the one at Hoddesdon dominated the room. No fire burned in the hearth and a raised dais had been constructed before it. The hall was alive with a great bustle of activity as nearly one hundred men from every station of life seemed intent upon making their voices heard.

"That's the Lord Mayor of London, Sir Stephen Soane," Green explained, pointing to a figure on the dais. Soane was splendidly attired in an elaborate wig and robes. "And those around him are the famous and well-to-do of the city. The front ranks are the men of business: Sir John Hart, Richard Cockayne, Thomas Hudson and there, to his left, see the balding man? That is the man we have come to speak with, Sir Thomas Smythe. Those men control not only the merchant life of the City, but countless other matters from the price of a quarter-lamb in the Stock's Market to the doings of a vessel in the seas of the Indies."

Sweeping his hand back, Greene indicated the men of the sea filling the body of the hall—sturdy captains and rugged sailors, eager for any new venture. "Look, Robert. The thin man? He is James Lancaster, captain of our first trading venture to the Moluccas. 'Tis said only 25 of his 200 men survived the three-year voyage and that Lancaster wept with every death.

"And by his side, that is John Davis, explorer of much of the northern lands and inventor of the backstaffe and double quadrant."

Bylot's heart leapt to see the famous explorers he had read so much about. Here, in the same room as him, were the men he hoped to emulate. Bylot had made the right decision following Greene.

A man beside Davis caught Bylot's attention. He was of middling years, with a long face, sharp features and a small pointed beard. Even in the crush of the hall, he was wearing a green outdoor coat with a dark fur collar.

"Who's the man in the green coat?" Bylot asked.

"I know not," Greene replied, dismissively, "but he is of no account. There are many who hang on to the coattails of the famous.

"What is more to our purpose is that these men are touted as being the best to lead a new expedition to the east. And you will be honoured to sail with them."

"Sail with them?"

"Of course. You wish for a life on the sea, do you not?"

"Yes," Bylot said hesitantly. He had not expected things to move as quickly, and he was daunted by the activity and the importance of all the dignitaries.

"Then this is the place to be and this is the night to be here. There are great adventures in the offing and chances aplenty for advancement.

"Look yonder," Greene instructed, pointing to a far corner of the hall. "See the rough crew by the door?" Robert nodded as he examined a dozen or so scarred veterans of who-knew-what thrilling adventures. "They are men from Drake's crew, come to examine these proceedings. Some sailed with Fenton and Hawkins, too."

As Bylot scanned the tumult in the hall, his eye fell on a figure near the back. He was of great age, as witnessed by his long beard and white hair. His skin was much wrinkled and pallid, but his eyes sparkled as they swept around the room. The man was dressed in a threadbare long cape and carried a silver-handled staff. Although surrounded by a crush of people, he managed to stand aloof from the proceedings. It appeared as if those around him drew back ever so slightly, creating a space, small but significant, around his shape.

"Who's that?" Bylot asked, pointing.

"I cannot know all . . . ," Greene's voice dropped when he saw who Bylot was pointing at. Pulling down his companion's arm, he continued, "That is Doctor John Dee, the Magus—mathematician, astrologer, geographer, friend to Her Majesty and man of many talents and interests."

"He looks frail."

Greene laughed. "Frail? I think not. Dee's interests include alchemy and the magic arts. He has sought the Philosophers' Stone—the substance that can turn lead into gold—and has communicated with the angels through crystal gazing. Some even say he has discovered the elixir of life itself. Do not be fooled by his outward appearance, his is the greatest mind of our age.

"Dr. Dee has many and varied connections. You will be lucky if your paths cross. He has much knowledge of use to one who wishes to learn the navigational arts."

As Greene talked, Bylot kept his gaze on Dee. He could easily imagine the thin, bird-like form hunched over smoking beakers and glowing crystal orbs within which vague forms solidified and melted. Suddenly, Dee's head snapped around and his eyes fixed upon Bylot. The man was fully fifty feet away and looking over a sea of chattering heads; nonetheless, the effect was startling. Bylot's head jerked back in shock at the intensity of his gaze. For an instant, he thought he felt Dee's eyes burn into him and he had the strangest feeling that Dee knew who he was. Then it was past, Dee was looking again at the front of the hall where Thomas Smythe was now addressing the throng.

Smythe was not a tall man, and was not as ostentatiously dressed as some, but he was a man of presence. "Listen well," Greene hissed. "This man has influence and power. He directs both the Levant and Muscovy Companies, and has the ear of the Queen herself." Smythe's voice was not loud, but it had a carrying quality and, as he spoke, the noise died away and men listened.

"Since Cornelius Houtman's return these two years past," he began in summary, "fifteen Hollander companies have taken interest in commercial voyages to the Moluccas. At present, this is to our advantage. Their resources are spread between the companies and consequently the profits small. However, I have heard talk of amalgamation into one large company. If that be the case, then our interests would be severely threatened.

"Already, as you know, the Hollanders feel secure enough in their control of their trade source in the Indies to have raised the price of pepper on the Amsterdam docks from three shillings per pound to eight." A grumble of discontent rolled around the hall.

"This iniquity has dealt a hard blow to all honest merchants who trade in this commodity. Thus we have met to determine an appropriate response. I have been most gratified at the discussions I have heard this night."

"They meet tonight," Greene's voice hissed in Bylot's ear, "to petition Her Majesty to allow them to set up a company to rival the Hollanders in the trade of spices. It is a daunting undertaking—the Hollanders will not give up their trade easily—but the benefits are limitless."

Bylot's attention swung back to Smythe, who was calling for a vote. "So, we are all of a mind to petition Her Majesty for a charter to be called the Governor and Company of Merchants Trading to the East Indies?" Heads nodded throughout the hall. "We have an honourable fifteen directors with my humble self as governor, and we have raised a subscription to purchase and outfit a fleet of sturdy vessels to sail to the East and purchase such quantities of pepper and other diverse spices as may be had from the local potentates. All those in favour of this venture—"

A forest of hands shot up and a great roar of agreement filled the hall. Nodding with satisfaction, Smythe returned to his seat. Sir Stephen Soane now stood and, although few could hear him, drew the meeting to a close. Bylot glanced at the back of the hall. There was no sign of Dee.

"Come, now is our chance," Greene said, grabbing Bylot by the arm and hauling him against the current of bodies streaming for the doors. After a few minutes of struggle, the pair stood before Smythe. Close up, Bylot was less impressed with the man. His fleshy face was scarred with old pox, a feature Smythe tried to hide by the liberal application of powder, and his full lips were wet with spittle. Nevertheless, he was still an imposing figure. His pale blue eyes held the men who fawned their congratulations around him for brief moments before dismissing them by moving on.

"Sir Thomas," Greene said deferentially. "A masterfully handled occasion, if I may be so bold."

Smythe, a fixed half-smile on his face, ignored Greene and stared hard at his companion. The watery eyes missed nothing. Bylot felt like a bug under a lens.

"This is Robert Bylot," Greene went on. "An untried youth, but one set to make his mark on the world of commerce and adventure."

"Have you experience of sailing, lad?" Smythe asked.

"Not yet, sir," Bylot replied, stepping forward. "But I am eager to learn, given the opportunity."

"That is good, but as you can see from the collection of sea dogs here today, there is no shortage of experience for this venture. My advice would be to attend a school hereabouts, pick up mathematics and the arts of navigation. Practise those arts on shorter voyages around our coasts and then return to present yourself once more."

It took a moment for Bylot to realize he was being dismissed. "I can learn on the voyage to the Moluccas," he stammered, too late. Already, Smythe was speaking to someone else.

Bylot turned to seek help from Greene, but his new companion was no longer beside him. Bylot craned his neck to see over the crush of heads, but there was no sign of Greene. Had this meeting been a cruel trick, designed to embarrass him? But why? What did Greene stand to gain?

Bylot pushed his way through the crowd, his emotions taking another turn on the day's roller coaster—his father's death, the journey, London, meeting Greene, the doubt, the excitement of the meeting and now the confusion of abandonment.

Out on the street, Bylot looked over the small groups of men standing around by the flickering light of flaming torches. He searched their faces, but there was no sign of Greene. What was he to do? He was exhausted. As he looked around helplessly, someone spoke.

"Perhaps I may be of some small assistance." The voice was soft, yet it carried clearly over the hubbub around them. Bylot turned to see John Dee regarding him with hooded eyes. Close up, he appeared even more aged. Deep canyons criss-crossed his cheeks, and surrounded his eyes and mouth in intricate patterns. Oddly, the sibilant voice that issued from the thin lips sounded much younger than its owner looked. Bylot's heart lurched as he imagined that this man had indeed drunk the elixir of life and was now destined to live an eternity in this withered body.

"It is but little surprise that Smythe was of no help—he has the narrow vision of a man of business. The broader world with all its variety escapes a mind dedicated to commerce. But excuse me. My name is John Dee—"

"I know," Bylot blurted out.

Dee nodded acknowledgement. "I see that even in the twilight of my years, I am not invisible to a new generation. And it is a new generation that I seek.

"If you indeed know of me, then you know that much of my life has been dedicated to the idea of an Empire to rival Rome, but with England at its heart. In my modest ways, I have used what influence I have to that end. Drake, Davis, Hawkins, even that rogue Frobisher, all benefited from my advice and influence. But that generation is done. In part it was my fault. In my naive youth I thought that the way to my imagined Empire was through commerce. To that end, I aided the likes of Smythe with his Muscovy Company and other ventures. My misjudgment was in underestimating the power of money to corrupt even the fairest ideals. Voyages that should have had the purest motives were debased by the lure of gold, just as the traitorous Spanish and Portuguese explorations have been. On the verge of great things, vulgar profit has overwhelmed the eyes and hearts of the sturdiest explorer."

Bylot stood, his jaw drooping, struggling to take everything in.

"I see now that naught of value to my aims can be gained through the offices of men such as Smythe. In the time I have left to me, I hope to pass on my knowledge and hopes to a younger, purer generation. I shall not live to see their achievements but, I am convinced, they shall far outstrip the petty discoveries of commerce.

"You, lad, are just the sort I seek. What I propose is to establish you in my property at Clerkenwell to learn the mathematics of navigation. What say you?"

Bylot's mind reeled. Here he was being offered tutoring in exactly the arts he sought, by the greatest mind of the age. But why? He had followed Greene and been abandoned. What should he do here?

"I don't know," Bylot replied helplessly.

"Then perhaps you are not for my small school after all." Dee began to turn away.

"Wait," Bylot spoke hurriedly. He was near collapse and the alternative was slumping into a filthy doorway. At least Dee didn't seem the sort who would slit his throat for a few pennies. "I was hasty. I am new in the city and much confused. I am honoured by your offer."

Dee returned his gaze to Bylot. "Good. Then we must make haste. It is late."

Dee strode off down the road, with Bylot scrambling after. The Magus made no allowance for people already in the street, but all moved aside to let him pass, some even crossing themselves as they did so. At the corner, as Dee ushered Bylot into his curtained carriage, Bylot thought he caught a glimpse of Henry Greene, watching from the deepening darkness. But he had no time for investigation. A word from Dee, a crack of the whip from the driver and the carriage was in motion.

# 3

# The Alchemist's Lair

Bylot and Dee travelled in silence, behind the carriage curtains, out to the northern fringes of the city. Eventually, the carriage stopped under the old Roman city walls, and they dismounted and entered a narrow, foul-smelling alley. At the far end stood a large house of great age. It had obviously been standing long before the stinking street had grown around it, but retained little of the grandeur that it once must have possessed. As Bylot followed Dee down the alley, he noticed how the local inhabitants cast furtive glances, both fearful and angry, at his companion. They even seemed to draw back as the pair passed. One old hag pushed forward a begging claw, but withdrew hurriedly at Dee's hiss.

Dee led the way to a side door that opened into a long corridor lit by torches set in black iron holders on the bare stone walls. "This is my town house," he explained. "I am fortunate enough to also possess a country estate at Mortlake, far from this cramped squalor, but it is convenient to undertake some of my work in the city.

"I have private rooms above, but this floor," Dee swept his arm wide in a gesture that took in the rows of doors leading off to each side, "is let to my apprentices and teachers. You shall sleep here. But first I would show you the workshops in the undercroft."

Dee lifted a torch from the wall, indicated that Bylot should do the same, and led the way through a narrow archway and down some heavily worn steps.

The undercroft was a low room, with a barrel-vaulted ceiling made from flat, reddish bricks. It exhibited none of the dampness usual in such underground lairs. The floor was made of an intricate pattern of black and white tiles that, although they were laid perfectly flat, gave Bylot the unsettling sense of being in three dimensions.

"To go down is to go back in time," Dee said as he led the way into the centre of the room. "This was once the bathhouse of a magnificent villa. The Roman lord who lived here controlled the entire island of Britannia and answered to none but Caesar Augustus himself. He took his leisure in the warmth that rose from pipes and cavities beneath the floor, unfortunately now much decayed and collapsed."

The walls around Bylot were stacked with books and rolled manuscripts of all sorts and sizes—from huge, leather tomes to tiny pocket volumes. Some exuded an aura of great age, a theory that was supported by the musty smell in the air.

Two armchairs were positioned beside a large fireplace, on whose mantle sat all manner of oddly shaped crystals and glasses, and a human skull. A vast oak table took up most of the floor space. On its surface were scattered documents and volumes open to a bewildering array of strange drawings and texts. In the centre of the table sat a large, magnificently ornamented globe.

Bylot's father had owned a small library, but it was nothing compared to this extraordinary room. Bylot wished Evelyn were here to see it.

"Knowledge is power," Dee said as he strode to the fire and poked it into life. "That is what I seek and what I have collected here. And that is what, if you are willing and able, I shall impart to you."

Bylot wandered the room, peering at the volumes lit by his blazing torch. Most were completely unfamiliar, but he recognized some authors from his studies—Aquinas, Duns Scotus, Boethius. Other names—Pelagius, Peter of Abano, Henricus Agrippa—meant nothing. Many sported odd titles—*De Occulta Philosophia, Thesaurus Spiritum, de daemonibus*—and a few—*Perfect Arte of Navigation* and *Propaedeumata aphoristica*—bore Dee's own name. Several titles were little more than collections of symbols, both mathematical and arcane, and some had odd drawings of winged beasts and flying demons.

One book on the table, lying open at a picture he recognized, caught Bylot's eye. The picture, crudely yet vividly drawn, showed scenes from Revelations, mostly concerning the signs of the coming apocalypse. The text was in a foreign tongue, but beside it lay parchments covered with scrawled English, obviously a translation in progress. Bylot lifted the book and regarded the cover. The title, *The Necronomicon*, was unfamiliar, but a shiver ran down his spine as he read it.

Dee gently removed the book from Bylot's hands, closed it and replaced it on the table by the globe. "You are not yet ready. You must walk before you can fly, young Bylot. But come, place your torch in the bracket and look at this: it is more in keeping with your learning.

"Navigation is the knowledge of the future. England is destined to be the centre of a great Empire that will stretch across the whole world—it is in the stars and the proofs go back to the ancient kings. You may be a part of that future if you wish, and if you apply yourself to your studies."

Dee led Bylot over to a great globe. He rested his aged hand almost lovingly on the swirls and indents of the complex coastlines. "This is Master Molyneux's globe—the first made in England. It is the sum of all our knowledge of this world we inhabit."

Bylot leaned closer, examining the globe. It was a masterpiece of detail and accuracy. Bylot had seen many maps in his studies, but they had been crude things, showing only the coarsest features. They had been enough to give him a good sense of the world and what was known and what was not, but they were nowhere near the quality of this wonder. Bylot felt like an angel, looking down upon the earth from heaven. But the more he looked, the more he saw that the apparent accuracy was simply extraordinarily good draughtsmanship. This map incorporated information from the recent voyages of Drake, de Gamboa, Cavendish and Davis, yet even with his meagre knowledge of geography, Bylot could see that this was mixed with the older, questionable geographies of Zeno. The globe was not, as it claimed in the title inscribed in the ocean beside England, "a true, hydrographical description of so much of the world as has been hereto discovered and come to our knowledge." Rather, it retained much that was dubious from previous thinking and even introduced some new doubts.

"Have you attended school?" Dee asked conversationally.

"I have. The local grammar school in Hoddesdon."

"And did you attend well to your lessons?"

"As well as I could," Bylot replied, remembering with a twinge of sadness how carefully he had tried to remember things so he could share them later with Evelyn.

"Tell me what you see here," Dee asked, waving his hand over the North Atlantic.

"I see Scotia, Finmarc and Icelandia fairly represented. This *Meta Incognita* must, certainly, be Greenland," Bylot ventured, leaning closer, "and, if so, then Queen Elizabeth's Foreland and Frobisher's Strait are transposed most magically across the Strait of Davis."

Dee laughed. "You are a sharp observer, young Bylot. You have an interest in explorers and the shape of our world?"

"I do. I have read whatever books I could find on the voyages of exploration. My favourite is Master Hakluyt's *Principal Navigations*."

"Excellent! Then name for me the four families of maps."

Bylot's mouth went dry and his mind blank. He was being tested. "Times of stress are when the mind should be sharpest," Dee said, observing his new student closely. "Fear is the greatest human weakness, but it is most often of little consequence.

"You fear me now because you are the student and I the teacher, and I have set you a test. But think on this. In but a few years time, if you persevere, you will be in your prime. I, on the other hand, if I am not rotting in a casket, shall be a drooling idiot needing to be spoon fed and wiped by others."

Bylot began to protest, but Dee held up a hand. "Do not deny what is inevitable. I have no elixir of life—that was but a pipe dream of youth. I shall rot the same as any man and, if we outlive our span as I have done, the rot begins before we reach the tomb.

"Seek to overcome your fear, young Bylot. Dwell not on it but think on something plain, such as the next breath you must draw whether you fear or not."

Bylot struggled to follow what Dee was saying and, in doing so, calmed. With an effort of will he looked inward and felt the air rush in to fill his lungs. His mind went back to the classroom in Hoddesdon and the old teacher who had told him of maps and geography. He could see his teacher vividly, even smell the unwashed odour of old age that clung to the man. One by one, Bylot pulled up from his memory the descriptions of maps he had been taught and added his thoughts on each.

"There are the T-O maps, which show the world as interpreted from scripture. They are of no use to the practical traveller. They show the three continents—Europe, Africa and Asia—with the waters of the world around and between them and the Garden of Eden to the east, at the top."

Dee nodded encouragement.

"*Mappa mundi,* although the term is much misused these days, refer to more detailed versions of the T-O maps and include rivers and coastlines. Unfortunately, they are commonly so fanciful as to be of no real use."

Bylot closed his eyes to concentrate harder. "Then there are the portolan charts of the Mediterranean shores—limited in geographic scope, yet of great detail and much used by navigators around those shores.

"The fourth family are those great maps derived from the coordinates of Ptolemy. They are thought to show our whole world, complete as knowledge can make it."

"A good overview lad," Dee nodded his encouragement. "And what are rhumb-lines and what is the problem that necessitates them?"

Bylot's growing confidence vanished. "I don't know," he admitted.

"However much we know, there is always more knowledge to be gained," Dee said. "As you know, lines of longitude meet at the earth's poles." Dee traced lines toward the top and bottom of the globe. "This system works on a globe such as this, but on a navigator's chart—a flat map—the lines of longitude are parallel; they never meet. Now, since a ship sails over the surface of the globe with lines that meet and not on a flat chart, there is an error when a navigator plots his course on a map."

Bylot frowned with concentration. This was his first lesson and, despite the exhaustion in his bones, he didn't want to get it wrong.

"If a navigator plots his course over open ocean as a straight line on his chart, it will be wrong and he will miss his destination. Therefore, he must plot his course as a curved line—a rhumb-line."

Bylot nodded.

Dee unrolled a large map beside the globe and weighted down the corners with books. "This is Master Molyneux's globe transposed onto a sheet using Master Mercator's new projection. See, there are the rhumb-lines plotted on a flat chart."

Bylot allowed his finger to trace the curved lines across the world's oceans. "It is magical," he said in awe.

Dee laughed derisively. "There is nothing magic about

it. It is mathematics, and when you learn how to calculate your position on a ship at sea, you will curse the day you ever heard of rhumb-lines. But tell me, which of the maps you know would you like most to take with you on a voyage to unknown lands?"

"Either Master Mercator's chart, with all its errors and unknowns, or one of Claudius Ptolemy."

"What of a portolan?"

"That would be by far the best for navigation, but they cover only well-travelled areas around the Mediterranean and would be of no use for undiscovered realms."

Dee looked thoughtful for a moment. "That is what most think. But what if I were to tell you that I once observed a portolan of the whole world?"

"Impossible!" Bylot cried. A portolan of the entire world! No. The only way a chart such as that could be constructed was if someone had sailed everywhere and mapped it, and that was obviously wrong. No one had been to the poles or seen what unknown lands lay in the great southern ocean. "It must have been a forgery."

Dee smiled. "Do not be so ready to dismiss what you do not know or what does not fit with your ideas as impossible. Because something lies without our experience is a poor and arrogant reason for denying it. The chart I speak of was old and based on even more ancient knowledge. I am convinced it was genuine."

"What did it show?"

"Many wondrous things. Perhaps one day I shall share some with you. But for now, let us return to Master Molyneux. The errors that you so cleverly divine are of no great consequence. In fact, they may be to our advantage."

"How so? Surely the farther from the truth the map, the less use it will be?"

"Youth. Youth. Youth." Dee shook his head. "How I wish for the simplicity of such a world view and an honest belief in the absolute value, or even existence, of truth. The map's errors are of no consequence because I have the documents upon which they are based and so may draw my own conclusions. The errors are of use in that they may well confuse those who would wish to thwart our ends.

"I have the secret journals of Francis Drake." Dee waved his hand vaguely at the surrounding books.

"But they were not among the books at my school," said Bylot, confused. "They have never been published."

"Indeed," Dee smiled. "The pettiness of politicians who thought Drake's discovery of the western entrance to the Straits of Anian should be suppressed led to many lies and many secrets."

"Drake discovered the Straits of Anian?" Bylot could hardly believe his ears. He knew Drake had searched for the straits, but did not know he had found them.

"Not the entire passage," Dee went on. "He had no time to enter and navigate through, but he undoubtedly saw one end. I shall let you read the journals one day. And this one, too, which is its companion and speaks of the eastern end."

Dee produced a small volume from a hidden pocket in his cape. "These are the original journals of Master Davis from his three voyages to the icy realms. They indeed support your observations on Master Molyneux's map, but tell us of other, more important, things. What do you see on the map of a way through to the Straits of Anian?"

"Naught but that it must be far to the north, beyond the map's solid lines."

"Indeed, and remember this—solid lines are a map's great weakness as well as its strength. A confidently drawn line on a page carries a weight that bears no relation to the truth behind that line's location. A good draughtsman can draw entire continents with such conviction that all fall down in awe at his learning, yet there may be no more certainty to his sources than the wild imaginings of some long-dead charlatan out to create a name or foster some wild scheme. Always distrust solid lines, boy.

"Now, see here." Dee pointed to the coast of America, across Davis Strait from the tip of Greenland. The most obvious feature was the wide gash in the coastline made by the river mapped far inland by Jacques Cartier and the French. But Dee's finger rested to the north, where two indents in the coast ended in solid lines. "The two inlets. Can you read the names?"

Bylot peered at the fine script on the map. "Cumberland Strait is the northern one and below it, the Furious Overfall. The discoveries of Davis in 1587."

"Indeed. Lumley's Inlet is not shown, but it is of no consequence. Master Frobisher proved that it leads nowhere. Davis attempted passage of Cumberland Strait thrice and was each time blocked by solid ice that must certainly be anchored to some land mass forming the head of an inlet and blocking that route. That leaves but one possibility."

"The Furious Overfall?"

"Yes. That 'Great Sea falling down into the gulf with a

mighty overfall and roaring' as Davis called it. The way to Cathay that Davis himself characterized as a passage 'most probable, the execution easy.'"

"Why then did Davis himself not take it, and why is it shown here as a closed inlet?"

"Good questions both, but I think we have covered enough for a first lesson. I'll warrant you are in need of some sustenance and a soft bed for the night."

Bylot could not deny it. The adventures of the day were overwhelming him and he was having difficulty keeping his eyes open.

Dee led the way back upstairs where shouted instructions to a servant brought some bread and sausage. Bylot wolfed both down as Dee looked on.

Dee then led his guest into a room, sparsely furnished, but spread about with cushions and bedding. Candles were already lit and a fire flickered in the grate.

"I shall leave you now to your rest. On the morrow, your education begins in earnest."

And with that, Dee was gone. Bylot settled himself by the fire and thought over the events of the day. The morning when he closed his father's dead eyes and said farewell to Evelyn seemed an age ago rather than a few hours. How had his life changed so abruptly? Bylot had no idea, but before he could think about it in any detail, sleep overcame him.

# 4

## LEARNING

A fter the remarkable first day, life at Clerkenwell settled into a routine. Lessons were held in the main hall on the ground floor of the house. It was nowhere near as grand as the room Bylot had been to at Founders Hall. The wood panelling was cracked in many places, the hanging tapestries threadbare and the ceiling heavily blackened from smoke, although the fire was lit on only the coldest of days.

In winter, the handful of students and their teacher huddled at one end of the room, blowing on their fingers for warmth so that they could hold their quill pens. In summer they had to wrap rags around their heads to stop perspiration dripping onto the precious maps they were studying. Bylot's favourite season was fall, before it became uncomfortably cold, but after the rank summer smells of the surrounding alleys had eased.

To Bylot's disappointment, Dee did very little teaching himself, delegating most of the work to minions. For long periods, he was not in residence. But the Magus retained an interest in his charges and would appear without warning, a silent figure in black standing at the back of the classroom, observing. On one occasion, a student was disruptive of the lesson, arguing pointlessly for the archaic Catholic world view.

"Is it not folly," the boy had asked, "to presume to map the contours of the world for our own ends? Surely, the Lord placed Holy Jerusalem at the world's centre in mimicry of its place in heaven. Our duty is to fit what we see around us into His pattern. We can be no more sure of the evidence of our senses than we can the dreams of a fevered mind. All that can be known with certainty is God's word in the Good Book. Thus, should not our mapping efforts reflect this rather than our petty discoverings?"

The teacher, a hawk-nosed man from Switzerland with humourless Calvinist leanings, had ignored the question. So had Dee, but the following day, the student was gone.

There were never more than three or four students in attendance at any time and usually but a single teacher. Some of the latter had travelled from the continent to escape the continual religious disturbances there, and had to resort to teaching in their only common language—Latin. Most lessons, however, were undertaken in the language of Bylot's countrymen.

The primary focus of the lessons was mathematics and its applications to navigation. With the aid of John Davis's backstaffe, the students learned to read the sun at noon and the stars at night to determine their own position on the surface of the planet. They tramped the countryside triangulating every tree and bend in the river as they mastered the art of map making. But they were also taught geography, astronomy and italic script.

Life at Clerkenwell was sometimes hard. Dee was not a rich man and Bylot and the other students, and, he suspected, the teachers, had to shift for themselves. Fortunately,

Evelyn, whom Bylot corresponded with at every opportunity, sent him occasional sums of money from the Hoddesdon estate to keep him from starvation. She also told him about their father's funeral, the proposed sale of the Hoddesdon house and her approaching marriage. Bylot missed his sister terribly, but the learning took all his energy and he had no chance to visit her.

Bylot had enough money for his daily needs and, with care and a frugality that often left him with an aching stomach, he even managed to put some aside to purchase a few slender volumes to aid his studies and begin his own library. There were times during that first winter that Bylot was sorely tempted to forgo his book money in favour of a warm coat, but he persevered and developed a strong constitution that stood him in good stead in his later adventures.

Bylot developed a fascination for the world of learning he had entered. He absorbed every fact that was thrown at him and took to his lessons with enthusiasm, but his favourite subject was geography. He would spend whatever small amount of free time he had in Dee's great library, poring over maps and globes. They were all there, from Johannes Ruysch's *Universalior Cogniti Orbis Tabula*, with its fanciful Ptolomaic projections and the convergence of the newly discovered Americas and Cathay, to Mercator's wonderful *Atlas sive cosmographicae meditationes de fabrica mundi et fabricati figura* and Ortelius's less rigorous yet ever popular *Theatrum Orbis Terrarum*.

Bylot would sit for hours, tracing diverse coastlines with his finger and imagining the voyages of discovery that had determined them. In his mind he sailed with Drake,

Magellan, the Cabots, de Gama and a host of others, but one thing disturbed him in his explorations. Although there were common threads—Lok was influenced by Mercator, Mercator was influenced by Gemma and so forth—there was much disharmony in the way the coasts of the world were shown. Some of this was understandable, given that the geographers had to reconcile information from varied and often conflicting sources—Mercator, for example, never set foot beyond the narrow confines of his native Low Countries. Bylot reasoned that some attempts were more fantasy than reality, and that others were deliberately misguided to confuse and thwart trade competitors. But there was much that could be explained only by imperfect methods of study and a lack of knowledge. Mercator's masterful projection of the world was a giant step, but there were still many blind alleys and much *terra incognita* to be investigated.

In those hours with the maps and globes, Bylot determined what his life's work would be. He would resolve the difficulties in man's view of the world. He would not be a cartographer or engraver, but he would sail forth to the distant corners of the world and collect information of such precision that none could question its validity. In doing so, he would provide all that any engraver could wish for and be the source of such geographical notions that all maps would hereafter be called Bylots!

It was while he was engaged in such a fancy, one dull February day in 1601, that Dee entered the library. Without preamble, he told Bylot to meet him in five minutes by the carriage at the entrance to the alley. Puzzled by the summons, Bylot hurriedly did as he was told.

Once seated in the carriage with Dee, they set off through the city toward London Bridge. After a while, Dee spoke.

"Your learning goes well?"

"Indeed, yes. I have learned much in my time here and I would thank you for the opportunity."

Dee waved off Bylot's thanks. "Do you remember that first day you arrived? You asked two questions."

"I recall. I inquired that if the Furious Overfall is indeed the eastern entrance to the Straits of Anian, why did Davis not challenge the passage himself, and why was it shown as a closed inlet on Molyneux's map?"

"Very good. An accurate memory is a great gift to those who wish to know.

"The first of your questions is easily answered—Davis was frightened by the rush of ice and water from the Overfall. His ship was small and the chances of her being crushed by the ice high. It was an understandable decision, but not one that a founder of an empire would make. Great rewards always entail great risk.

"The second question is also simply dealt with, at least on the surface. The Furious Overfall is shown as a closed inlet because the map maker, or his backers, do not want the passage shown."

"Why?"

"Why, indeed. Therein lies the heart of the matter and of what I wish to discuss with you this day.

"The supporters of Davis, by which I mean Smythe and his ilk, are concerned that the riches of the Orient be theirs and theirs alone. The Portuguese, who are already there, pose little threat. They are a spent force in world affairs, and their ships are unwieldy and fall with remarkable ease to a few well-placed shots from our guns.

"The Hollanders are of greater concern. They are a rising power and are more a match for our vessels. However, they are but newly entered into the game and will be forestalled by a few well-placed fortresses. Thus security of trade—and this means almost exclusively trade in spices with the potentates of the Moluccas—depends upon securing the routes to the source.

"Now, there are but five routes from fair England to the Moluccas, two known and three unknown."

"The route of de Gama around Africa," Bylot said in response to Dee's questioning glance. "The route of Magellan around the southern continent of the Americas. And the northern routes—direct across the Pole, around Muscovy, and by the Straits of Anian at the northern terminus of the Americas."

"Excellent. Now, which would you take to reach Cathay?"

Bylot's learning popped easily into his mind and he answered without any of the nerves he had felt eighteen months before. "De Gama's is the surest, but it is long and arduous and there are many perils in the Hollanders and Portuguese who would prey on English ships." Dee nodded encouragement as they bumped along the highway. "Magellan's route, by Drake's own account, is fraught with dangers and reef-laden waters. That leaves but the three northern routes, and I know little of them.

"The route by the Pole is unknown," Bylot continued, "but it depends upon there being open ocean in those far northern climes and, despite the arguing of some around the quantities of sunshine thereupon, all evidence indicates that the ice becomes more of an obstacle the farther north one progresses.

"The Muscovy route I do know has taken many a brave soul, Willoughby and Barents among them, and I fear the passage there might be no less arduous than Magellan's Strait. Of the route by the northwest, I can find but small difficulty and in truth I am much puzzled by the lack of progress in that realm."

"Splendid! Splendid!" Dee clapped a claw-like hand on his companion's knee. "You have a sharp mind, young Bylot. It will serve you well if it does not kill you first. The passage to the northwest is my own thinking exactly. As to your puzzlement, that is understandable. It took me many years to realize what was happening. But first, I think it is time I outlined my thinking to you."

Bylot tensed in anticipation. Here was what he craved even more than the book learning in which he had been immersed—the knowledge and perspective of the Magus himself.

"We are either privileged or damned to live in such interesting times. I do not believe, as some do, that the Apocalypse is nigh; yet there are troubles aplenty to occupy us all. England has been spared many of the wars and famines of our continental neighbours. In my travels I have seen entire populations living in abject fear of the next marauder who will pass by. We have escaped that, in part because of our isolation as an island, but in the main because we are destined."

"Destined?" Bylot asked into the pause that followed.

"Yes!" Dee's grip tightened and he turned on the seat and gazed hard at Bylot. "Destined to usher in a new age. Do you know your history?"

"Some," Bylot replied, part confused, part concerned by the turn the conversation was taking.

"And that you have in common with most folk from the poorest peasant to the mightiest lord. We know only a partial history. There is another, a deeper history that only a select few are privileged to understand. I, through a lifetime of toil and searching, am one. You, I have chosen to be another."

Dee relaxed his grip, sat back in the carriage and directed his gaze out the window at the river. It seemed as if the conversation was over. Bylot sat in silence. Was a response expected? Had he missed some meaning?

"Thank you," he said weakly.

Dee laughed—a thin, rattling sound. "Do not thank me. It is not a favour or a bauble I hand on to you, but an awesome responsibility. And with responsibility comes struggle, hardship and toil. Perhaps only death lies in wait at the end, but perhaps success and glory barely imaginable. Perhaps your name will be remembered in the Pantheon of the great empire makers—Alexander, Caesar, Bylot. It is a heady thought is it not?"

Bylot remained silent, his head reeling. What was this all about? He wasn't an Alexander or a Caesar.

"But we are far from that yet," Dee went on, "and first you must understand what has gone before and why destiny calls now.

"It is my firm belief, grown from long study of rare and ancient books, that our world is corrupt. That we have deviated from our intended course and that is why we are sinking ever farther into chaos and nightmare. It was not always so. There was a time when all was harmony and mankind marched forward to a golden future, united and secure. All our scrabbling after knowledge is but a pitiful attempt to regain something of what was known by the ancients in a time when all wisdom was one and lead could indeed be transformed into gold."

Dee paused. When he resumed, his voice was almost wistful. "How many years did I waste chasing that alchemist's trick?"

Dee smiled at the look of shock on Bylot's face. "Aye, lead into gold is but a trick—a conjuror's artifice to entertain the rabble. The mistake is in realizing that, alone, the trick is meaningless. The broader wisdom of the ancients must be regained, then all lead will be gold."

Beneath his hooded eyes, Dee's gaze held Bylot enthralled. "Humankind was strong then—a straight trunk reaching ever upward for the stars. But then came a split. A branch grew out from the main trunk. It grew and swelled until no one could tell that it was not itself the trunk. The original trunk was forgotten and it withered. The new branch did not grow strong and straight, but wound its way to the side. And then it split and the split branches split again, until we were lost in a forest of ever smaller branches that intertwined and grew every which way but up. Until we return to the original trunk and revitalize it, we cannot hope to regain the stars. My destiny, and yours, is to return to the main trunk."

Bylot sat in long silence, agonizing beneath Dee's penetrating stare. He desperately wanted to ask Dee what it all meant, but he was frightened of appearing stupid in front of this man who put so much trust in his abilities. "When did this branch grow out?"

"I see you begin to understand." Dee nodded. "The branch grew out—and we began to move away from God and His purpose, losing ourselves in the confusion—when mighty Troy fell to the Greek hordes of King Agamemnon.

"Priam of Troy was the last great king and his line stretched back to the dawn of mankind. They ruled in a Golden Age, an age of mighty palaces with painted walls and halls linked by stairways of a thousand steps, set amidst groves of olives and grapes. They were a beautiful people, their fair faces untroubled by disquiet or worry. They strolled through their days in careless pursuit. For entertainment, the women sang in wondrous voice and brave youths leapt upon the backs of bulls.

"All this was possible because the world was one. There was no need for cyclopean walls surrounding cities or for armies and navies to do battle with enemies—there were no enemies. It was an Eden rich in blessings.

"But there was a worm in the apple. Newcomers, coarse in manner and dress, came from the north and settled amidst the people. The land they cultivated was hard—cold in winter and dry in summer—but they had everything they could want, their shortcomings of food in bad years being cheerfully met by their better-situated neighbours. However, jealousy grew in their hearts. Why could they not have the best and be the ones to generously distribute their excess bounty? They were a small tribe so they could do naught but nurse their growing resentment.

They were the Greeks—the Attic peoples, they were called then."

"But weren't the Greeks the fathers of all our thought?" Bylot asked. "Don't all our ideas stem from them?"

"They do," Dee replied, "and that is the difficulty. But you get ahead of yourself. I am talking of a time long before Athens and the Parthenon, and of a people who make the vaunted Greek philosophers—Aristotle, Plato and the rest—seem merely questioning children.

"At this time, there came troubles—mighty earthquakes shook down the glorious palaces, fire rained from the sky and giant waves flooded the land. Amidst all this suffering, the Attics saw their chance. Like a plague that strikes on the heels of famine when things are at their worst, the Attics beat their farming tools into strong armour and weapons, and swept out of their poor land to ravage the destroyed palaces. They pillaged wherever they went and took what they needed, settling their own people on the fertile land they stole.

"The ancients tried to respond, learning the arts of defensive war as best they could, but they were no match for the invaders. Only one group succeeded. Led by a young king, they retreated across the seas and built a huge impregnable city on a plain—Troy. For generations, they lived there, remembering the old ways and defeating all who came against them while the rest of the world fell into turmoil and conflict.

"At length, the Attic peoples realized that they could never be truly secure while Troy survived as a beacon of what used to be. So, in an unprecedented move, they united and waged a mighty war—a war told of by Homer. After ten long years, the Attics triumphed by subterfuge and holy Troy was destroyed, but some escaped. Aeneas was one; he had a son and a grandson and a great-grandson. The last's name was Brutus and he led a small band of Trojans to these shores of Britain. Here he defeated the mighty Gog and Magog and built Troia Nova, whose remains lie buried deep within the London clay.

"Brutus and his men were too few to resurrect the Golden Age. All they could do was remember. This they did while wild savages battled around them. Then came the Romans. For four hundred years a weak copy of the Golden Age existed, yet it was too self-serving and subject to man's whims. The descendants of the Trojans waited, generation upon generation.

"When the Romans left Britain, a king called Arthur felt the time right for a new dawn, but he was wrong. Nevertheless, even though he failed, Arthur's legacy was a light that shone through the dark ages. That is the power of an idea.

"Now, the time is right."

Dee fell silent and his gaze wandered again out the carriage window as it rattled beneath the arch through Nonesuch House and across London Bridge. Bylot barely knew what to say. He had understood Dee's words, but the story was so fantastic. "How did you learn all of this?"

"There are sources, young Bylot. Some obvious, Geoffrey of Monmouth's *Historia Regum Britanniae* for one. There are others; forgotten books. If one is diligent they can be found. For the idea of Troy and the Golden Age to be kept alive some things must be written down."

"Why is now the right time?"

"Because the world is changing. There is a new interest in learning. The old ways are being challenged on every hand—people are questioning the power of the church, kings and emperors are being brought down everywhere, and new ideas are being put forward daily. Of course, there is a misplaced belief that it is the so-called classical world—the very world of the Attics whom I despise—that is fuelling this new birth, but that is no matter. The truth will soon be seen."

"How? Do you mean to publish these forgotten books?"

"Ah, no. To do that would simply put ancient wisdom on the same footing as every other new idea that pours forth from Master Gutenberg's commendable invention. What must be done is to create an example—a shining beacon that cannot be ignored and which every man will want to emulate. That torch shall be the Empire of England across the seas."

Bylot gasped. Suddenly, he understood Dee's interest in navigation. It wasn't just to discover the unknown places of the world for their own sake; it was to foster and encourage the idea of a new Golden Age, led by England.

Oblivious to Bylot's enlightenment, Dee continued. "My studies have firmly established our right to the new lands of America through the voyages and colonies of Prince Madoc many years before that Genoese upstart, Christof Columbo, was even an infant on his mother's teat. It is our destiny to take the northern lands and create a new world there for all to admire and envy. Then they will flock back and beg to be shown the ancient wisdom.

"My error was in thinking that this could be achieved through commerce. It is not so. Commerce is its own master and cares for naught but immediate profit. Frobisher and the rest were but pawns in Smythe's game. To discover a pure new land, the motives of the voyagers must themselves be pure. That is what *you* shall be, lad—a knight of the new order sallying forth under sail to discover a new world that will be the foundation of a return to the Golden Age and the birth of our salvation."

Bylot sat in awe. If he had indeed understood Dee's words, a dreadful responsibility was being placed upon his shoulders. He opened his mouth to deny the new role that was being thrust upon him, but the carriage jerked to a sudden stop and he was thrown forward across the seat.

"Take care, lad," Dee said over his shoulder as he opened the door and alighted. "You must develop better sea legs than that for your venture. Now come and see a sight you shall not soon forget."

Embarrassed by his clumsiness, Bylot struggled out of the carriage. They had stopped at the dockside in Southwark, hard by the square tower of St. Saviour. Before the two men lay the mighty river spanned by the great bridge. On the far shore was the skyline of London, the greatest city in the world and, if Dee were to be believed, heir to Troy.

The bank was crowded with sightseers, many in the livery of high-born estate. All gazed out across the water where four ships were just beginning to hoist sail and catch the wind. They were a magnificent sight; each high-sided hull was luminous with glaring red, blue and black checkered and diamond patterns, and every mast was heavy with multicoloured bunting, streamers and pennants. Each ship also flew a giant blood-red cross of St. George.

"The *Ascension*—32 crew; *Susan*—82; *Hector*, I delight in the irony of the Trojan name—108; and *Red Dragon*—202." Dee listed the ships from smallest to largest. "The first commercial venture of the Honourable East India Company. In command, James Lancaster, first pilot, John Davis. Objective: to secure a profit, either by trade or plunder, it matters little."

"Oh, it matters." Dee and Bylot turned to see Thomas Smythe smiling at them. "Plunder is much the preferable alternative. No initial outlay and we confound Her Majesty's enemies."

"My apologies, Sir Thomas. I forget some of the subtleties of the commercial world. I assume that explains the great guns on the *Red Dragon*."

"Indeed. We cannot send brave men off to the farthest corners of the world lacking in adequate protection. This is a practical venture, not some theoretical search for an earthly paradise."

"And that is why the benefit will accrue to only you and the directors, not the English people."

Smythe's smile didn't waver. "Aye. To the 215 men with guts enough to put their hard-won £72 000 where their mouths are." His gaze left Dee and settled on Bylot. "I know you, lad?"

"Aye, sir," Bylot said, stepping forward and offering his hand. "My name is Robert Bylot. I approached you at the meeting in Founders Hall, some eighteen months ago."

"Bylot," Smythe said thoughtfully, making no move to take Bylot's hand. "You are the lad who wished a life on the sea?"

"Aye, sir," Bylot repeated, withdrawing his hand in embarrassment. "Dr. Dee is teaching me navigation."

Smythe laughed shortly. "And much more too, I'll warrant. Is he filling your head with all his nonsense of Troy and a Golden Age?"

"I but give the boy a broader view of the world than that seen by narrow money grubbers," Dee answered icily.

Bylot shrank back, watching the two men verbally spar. There was obvious dislike on both sides.

"Narrow is it?" Smythe retorted. He waved his arm to encompass the river scene. "There is the narrow view of commerce. *That* is the future, John Dee. Lancaster and Davis will return with holds filled with spices and they are but the first. Trade is the way to fashion an empire."

"Well," Dee said softly. "I wish them more luck than Lancaster had on his previous voyage. I hear he left many more corpses in the Moluccas than he brought home on his disease-ridden ships."

"I am sure they would be grateful for your wishes, but they have no need of them. Sickness will not be a problem. Lancaster carries several bottles of lemon juice to feed to his crew. He believes it to be efficacious against the scurvy."

"Lemon juice!" Dee scoffed. "Much good will that quack panacea do him. Scurvy results from the miasma that builds when too many men are confined in unhealthy quarters. Lancaster would do better to ventilate below decks."

The pair were interrupted by a cheer as the *Red Dragon* fired her guns in a farewell salute. With billowed sails and streaming flags, the small, colourful armada caught the racing tide in the middle of the river and began their journey.

"Well, they are off," Smythe said, "as must I be. I bid you good day, Dr. Dee, and you too, Master Bylot. Perhaps if you concentrate on your mathematics, I might have use of you one day."

Smythe turned and rejoined a group of well-dressed men standing on the river bank. All were in high spirits, clapping each other on the back and talking loudly. A man in the crowd caught Bylot's attention—a familiar thin figure darting between the dignitaries. Bylot frowned in concentration. Then it came to him. Henry Greene! The crowd shifted and Greene vanished again, just as he had that night in Founders Hall.

Bylot turned to Dee to tell him about Greene, but the look on his teacher's face froze the words in his throat.

"Never," Dee snarled, "*never* fawn to the likes of that overblown slug. He cares naught for anything but the rich food he can put in his belly and the silk he can draw over it. Every word he utters is calculated to advance his own position, and every person he deals with is but a means to further his own ends." With a swirl of his cape, Dee swung around and strode toward the carriage. In shock at the harsh words, Bylot scuttled after him.

When they were both settled behind the carriage's drawn curtains, Dee spoke more calmly. "I brought you here to show you the beginnings of Smythe's adventure. I cannot say how it will end, but whether it be for better or no, nothing of real worth will accrue from it. My hopes for you are on an altogether higher plane."

The pair sat in silence on the journey back. Dee seemed distant and lost in thought. Bylot relived in his mind what he had seen and what he had been told. He would have to write it all down for Evelyn—the Golden Age of Troy that

Dee sought to recapture, the adventures of Brutus and the founding of London, King Arthur and his attempt to recreate the lost world. It all fit into a pattern and made a kind of sense, but was it true? Maybe, Bylot thought. He wished he could sit down and discuss it all with Evelyn—what a wonderful evening they would have with all Dee had told Bylot. For a moment, Bylot felt close to tears. All the talk of destiny, great empires and Golden Ages scared him. Sometimes he thought he would never be happier than he had been just learning things and discussing them with his sister.

But that wasn't completely true. The meeting with Smythe had left another small core of disappointment like a frozen ball in his stomach. Seeing Lancaster's expedition depart had reminded Bylot of his dreams of a life at sea. They hadn't come to anything yet. Would they ever? If he had gone about things differently, could he, at this moment, have been standing on the rolling deck of the *Red Dragon*? Certainly, Lancaster and Davies were simply following tried and true routes to the east, whereas Dee was offering a dramatically new approach. But perhaps tried and true was best—and safer. Bylot had learned much of great value in the past months, and Dee apparently had some spectacular venture in mind. But, Bylot wondered, was he really any closer to his goal than he had been outside Founders Hall?

As the carriage pulled up outside Clerkenwell, Dee roused himself from his reverie. "When I came to the library, I had another purpose as well. I had some news to impart. It seems your sister is ill."

"Evelyn? What's wrong? She was in good health when last she wrote."

"Apparently she is engaged to be married to some dunderhead and is not satisfied with her lot."

"Then I must go to her."

"Take care, young Bylot. Women are weak and subject to hysterics. It will not serve you well to go running after them whenever a vapour disturbs their equanimity. You have work to do here and I would not look kindly upon your desertion."

"How do you know about Evelyn's illness?"

"You received a communication." Dee pulled a letter from his pocket and handed it to Bylot. Robert's name was written on the front in a familiar hand, but the seal was broken.

"You read it!" Bylot exclaimed.

"I suspected it contained some information of note, and your work here is too important to be interrupted by petty concerns." Dee descended from the carriage and strode up the steps of the house.

Bylot sat, his mouth gaping in shock. Then he opened the letter and read.

*Dearest Robert,*

*I do not want to disturb you in your studies, but I write because I have no one else to turn too. My betrothal has become a sham and I am utterly alone. It has been much delayed by the settlement of the estate, which, as I have told you before, is more complex than we had hoped. I begin to suspect that this will turn out to be a blessing. David has begun to act monstrously as time*

*has gone by, and I know now that I cannot marry him.
I have always known he is a simple man without an
inquiring mind (such as yours), but I thought that with
the stability of marriage and the money I have brought
from father's estate (I have your share in trust), that I
would be allowed some freedom to pursue my interests.
It is not to be. David has made it abundantly clear that
he expects nothing of me other than to be his drudge and
the mother to a host of his brats. The very thought brings
on an attack of the fevers. He will permit no freedom,
either physical or intellectual, on my part. Last evening,
I pleaded with him most strongly, putting forward my
arguments with the logic you have taught me. It served
only to infuriate him to the degree that he raised his
fist and struck me a forceful blow across the cheek. It is
utterly hopeless and I will die before I live the kind of life
he expects of me. At the first opportunity, I shall escape,
to what I know not, but whatever my decision brings
will be better than a life of slavery. I am sorry to burden
you with my difficulties and will communicate again
when I can.
As always, my love,
Evelyn*

Bylot let the page slip from his fingers. His mind was a swirl of conflicting emotions: worry at Evelyn's situation, anger at Dee's interference and confusion at the day's happenings.

He sat for a long time before making a decision. Stepping down from the carriage, he entered the house, collected his meagre belongings and set out for the city gates. He might not be remembered with Alexander and Caesar, but he would help Evelyn.

# 5

## THE PLAGUE PIT

B ylot left the house at Clerkenwell with a strong sense of déjà vu. Eighteen months ago he had walked away from his father; now, he was walking away from Dee. But this time his step was light. Dee had taught him much, and he was grateful for it, but the Magus demanded total commitment. After their conversation in the carriage, Bylot wasn't sure he could give it. Now he could go where he wished and pursue the dreams *he* wanted.

Bylot spent his last few pennies on a bed in a rundown inn on the edge of the city and set off the following day over the downs toward Hoddesdon. It was a clear, frosty, February morning and the sharp air seemed to cleanse Bylot, washing away the mustiness of the dark rooms and alleys of Clerkenwell. Bylot was thrilled at the thought of seeing Evelyn again and almost ran the final miles, his booksack bouncing on his back.

His first view of the family house stopped Bylot in his tracks. In the less than two years he had been away, the house had aged—the garden was overgrown, ivy was over-whelming the west end, paint was peeling and a window to the right of the doorway was broken, the hole stuffed with rags. For a moment, Bylot was terrified that he had arrived too late, that something awful had happened to Evelyn, but then he relaxed. Of course the house was rundown. Evelyn was in the middle of selling it and settling the estate, and had told him she was living in rooms in town.

Bylot climbed the steps to the front door slowly. He was tempted to simply turn and go into town to seek out Evelyn, but the door was open and he felt he should check that everything was all right inside. The hallway was dusty and dark, and it took his eyes a minute or two to adjust to the gloom. As he stood, he heard a scraping noise coming from the corridor beside the main staircase. As quietly as he could, Bylot went to investigate.

Bylot's first view of Evelyn was of her back as she knelt in the corner, busily replacing the bricks that hid Bylot's bolt hole. He stood for a moment, content simply to be near his sister and happy just to watch. Eventually, Evelyn stood up and turned. She gave a little jerk of fright at the figure in the doorway, but it was instantly replaced by a squeal of recognition. "Robert!" she yelled as she hurled herself across the room and nearly knocked her brother over with the force of her embrace.

As the pair hugged, Evelyn rattled on. "You're here! I didn't expect you! Did you get my letter?" Eventually, she stepped back and looked at Robert sternly. "You haven't given up your studies, have you? I was just getting your old maps out of your 'library.'"

Bylot smiled. "I came to help ..." His smile faded as he noticed the livid, purple bruise on Evelyn's cheek. "David?"

Evelyn dropped her gaze and raised her hand to her face. "It's nothing. My fault, really."

"He hit you?"

Evelyn nodded, nervously. "He didn't mean to hurt me."

Bylot felt rage building inside him. "How do you hit someone in the face and not mean to hurt them? How dare he! You will not marry an animal like that. I will go and see him now." Bylot half turned.

"No!" Evelyn grabbed his arm. "There will be a fight. David has brothers. You will be hurt."

"But you cannot marry him."

"I know. I'm going to run away. That's why I'm here, to say goodbye." Evelyn raised her head and gazed at her brother. Her face was pale and tired, but her eyes sparkled. "Let's both go! I have some money and the estate is almost settled. We'll be able to live quite comfortably. We could go to London! You can continue your studies and I can keep house. You can show me everything you've seen and tell me all the things you've learned. It'll be just like old times."

Bylot's anger faded in the face of Evelyn's enthusiasm. It would be stupid to go and face David down. Only trouble would come of it and there would be no satisfactory resolution. Evelyn's idea was much more attractive, but was it possible? Bylot ran the idea round in his mind. Practically, it would work. The sale of Hoddesdon would provide enough money for them to live comfortably for many years. Bylot could continue his studies on his own or find other tutors. He would have enough money to buy books. Perhaps he could even go back and use Dee's library, although it would be very different dealing with the Magus if he were independent. When he was ready, Bylot could approach whomever he wished in the city to find employment. In addition to all that, he would be helping his sister.

"Yes," he said. "Let's go."

Evelyn hugged her brother so hard he felt his ribs were breaking.

That very afternoon, the pair, chatting aimlessly about future possibilities, walked to see the notary who was handling the sale of the house. As Evelyn had told Robert, the notary had a buyer and was happy to advance them some money against the final sale. With it, they hired a carriage, loaded what essentials they could from Hoddesdon, drove into town and found an inn for the night. After the best supper the innkeeper could provide, the pair sat by the fire exchanging news and talking excitedly about what they were going to do. Eventually, the innkeeper's obvious yawns drove them to retire.

Robert and Evelyn set themselves up in a modest house outside London's city walls. It was in Clerkenwell Parish, far enough from the noisome Green and the odorous River Fleet that it enjoyed some rural views and clear air, and yet was not too close to Dee's house.

One morning after they had settled in, Bylot plucked up his courage and went to see Dee. He was nervous about facing the Magus as he turned into the alley, but the sight that met him stopped him in his tracks. Dee's house, with its magnificent library, was a blackened ruin.

"What happened?" he asked an old man lounging against a wall.

"It be burned," the man said, spitting loudly onto the cobbles.

"How?"

The old man stared in silence. Bylot took a few pennies from his purse and held them out.

"Were a fire," the man said, staring greedily at the money. "'Bout three nights past. 'T'ain't nothin' left."

"How did it start?"

The old man shrugged and reached for the money. Bylot drew it back.

"'T'wer ruffians," the man said sourly.

"What became of Dee, the Magus?"

The man looked suddenly frightened. "Gone," he said, "and good riddance, too."

Bylot handed over the pennies and left. Some further inquiries established that three men had been arrested for starting the fire. No one had been injured, and Dee and the few students had gone. The fire probably wasn't too surprising, Bylot reflected, given the looks of fear and loathing that Bylot remembered on the faces of the alley dwellers when he first arrived. That evening, he discussed the events with Evelyn.

"The folk in the alley looked on Dee with fear," he said, as they sat by the fire. "The noises and lights from the laboratory frightened them and Dee encouraged that as a way to be left undisturbed."

"People will live in fear only so long," Evelyn commented. "Do you think the folk of the alley burned the house?"

"I would not be surprised if they had. I do regret the loss of his library, though."

"From what you have told me it was remarkable."

"It was. Some of the volumes were unique. Dee once showed me a part of Drake's secret journal."

"What did it say?" Evelyn's eyes gleamed with curiosity.

"It said that, in the summer of 1579, Drake voyaged to almost 58 degrees north above the coast of New Spain. He was turned back by icebergs and strong cold winds flowing from the icy mountains around. Nevertheless, he talked of much trade with the savages thereabouts and the suitability of the lands to the south, which he named Nova Albion, for settlement and agriculture.

"He believed that, at his farthest north, he had been in the western mouth of the Straits of Anian and, although Dee never showed me the calculations, he told me that Drake's readings indicated a mere 1,500 miles of passage to the Atlantic Ocean. Drake even dispatched a boat with a pilot and crew of twenty to sail home by that route, but some misfortune befell them and they were never seen again."

"Why have we not heard of this venture?"

"Because the documents were suppressed and the maps altered. The good queen and her ministers feared the Spanish would use the knowledge for their own ends."

"That's a disgrace!" Evelyn exclaimed angrily. "Knowledge of our world should be for everyone, not the benefit of a few. How is it that men of power take such a narrow, short view of such great events?"

Bylot smiled at his sister. Still angry over being denied an education because of her gender, Evelyn believed passionately in the freedom of all learning for any who should wish it.

As the months passed, Bylot and Evelyn settled into a comfortable routine. Many mornings, Bylot would go out to search for books. Others, he would sit in coffee shops or inns and read broadsheets and talk with the patrons. He would return with information and he and Evelyn would dissect it at length. He also spent many hours teaching his sister the rudiments of mathematics and geography that he had learned at Dee's school.

Evelyn absorbed the information like a sponge, and Bylot was continually surprised at her astute observations. She blithely dismissed Dee's talk of an English empire to rival that of the Trojans as wild imaginings, and had even less time for Smythe's plans of commercial ventures to the Moluccas.

"Neither will ever come to anything," she was fond of saying. "Dee's mysticism is nonsense. We are not placed here to fulfill some wild dream and recreate an imaginary world of the ancients. We simply do the best we can and hope that, at the end, we have, in some small way, improved mankind's lot by our efforts.

"As for Smythe's commercial ventures, they are doomed to fail. The driving force is not the benefit of man, savage or civilized, but the enrichment of a few already bloated merchants. To that end, they will murder and steal, and that can be no basis for a lasting empire."

Bylot could not completely accept his sister's arguments. Both Dee's wishes and Smythe's desires offered a chance for adventure and excitement that, however content he was with Evelyn, a part of him still craved.

Ψ

The pestilence first reared its head in the yards of Drury Lane in the spring of 1603. At the beginning, the disease seemed nothing more than a minor outbreak. The winter was hard that year and the river froze late, allowing the populace to cavort on its surface without a care. As the weather warmed, the weekly bills of mortality remained low, with an occasional hiccup in the squalid parishes of Shoreditch, Whitechapel and Cripplegate. But the bills were false; to prevent panic, many plague deaths that spring were reported as common ailments. By June, however, the deaths could no longer be explained as "griping of the guts" or "the bloody flox." The bills rose into the hundreds and the Lord Mayor introduced his *Orders Concerning the Infection of the Plague* and confined all with any connection to the distemper to their dwellings.

"Should we leave the city?" Evelyn asked.

"It would not be easy," Bylot countered. "Carriages are already extremely expensive, many roads are barred against refugees, and few towns or inns will accept a visitor from the city. We *could* return to Hoddesdon. We are known there and would be allowed to stay."

"No!" The violence of Evelyn's denial startled Bylot. "I shall not go back. I left and broke a contract for marriage. David could claim me under law and force me to be his wife. Anyway, we are most probably safe here. The disease will confine itself to the poorer parishes along the river, as it always has in the past."

Bylot had reservations, but he allowed himself to be persuaded by his sister's arguments. So they stayed, taking what comfort they could in pamphlets such as *Medela Pestilentiae* or *Necessary Directions for the Preventions and Cure of the Plague*.

In what they mistook for safety, Bylot and Evelyn sat like rabbits fascinated by a snake as the horror spread. They saw the new Scottish King James and the Court flee to Oxford. They watched as gaming, dancing, and music houses were closed, as much for lack of trade as a precaution, and as puppetry, rope dancing, Merry Andrew and all other street entertainments vanished. They scoffed as traders in charms and potions duped the gullible and as chalked incantations for protection appeared on neighbours' doors.

Some of the supplications were from the Psalms: "Surely He shall deliver thee from the noisome pestilence" and "Thou shalt not be afraid for the terror by night nor the pestilence that walketh in darkness" being popular, but the Bible was not the only source of comfort. Many people chalked magic charms and incantations. The word Abracadabra was often seen, written thus:

ABRACADABRA
ABRACADABR
ABRACADAB
ABRACADA
ABRACAD
ABRACA
ABRAC
ABRA
ABR
AB
A

Neither religious nor profane pleas had any effect.

All through that doleful summer, Bylot and Evelyn stayed indoors and hoped. At night, the bells of the dead-carts on their way to the burial grounds kept them awake. The bills of mortality rose until, in the hot months of July and August, nearly a thousand people were dying daily.

Ψ

One Sunday, late in September, Evelyn did not descend as usual to breakfast. Bylot climbed the stairs and knocked on her door.

"Come in," she said in a weak voice.

Bylot entered and found her still in bed, looking pale.

"I'm sorry," Evelyn said. "I don't feel well this morning."

A black fear enveloped Bylot and he found it difficult to suck enough air into his lungs.

"Don't look so shocked" Evelyn smiled weakly. "I have a slight fever. It's just a common cold. If I rest today, I shall be fine by supper."

Bylot nodded, not trusting himself to speak. All day he fussed over his sister, bringing cold towels to place on her brow and glasses of water to slake her thirst.

By evening, she seemed better, complaining of nothing more than a headache, and even descending to eat a light meal. Bylot allowed his hopes to soar. But they were cruelly dashed. On Monday the fever returned with renewed vigour and was followed by the appearance of the hideous swellings on Evelyn's neck and beneath her arms. There could now be no doubt. Bylot did what he could to ease his sister's pain, but it was nothing. With shocking rapidity the disease worked its destruction and by Tuesday afternoon the end was near.

"It is my fault we stayed," he said, holding her hand. "I should have insisted. We could have found some means to leave the city."

Evelyn lay back against her pillows, shallow breathing the only sign that life still resided in her ravaged form. Her eyes were closed and her features composed, although Bylot knew it was but a momentary respite. Beads of sweat stood out on her fevered forehead where livid red circles contrasted with her grey skin. On her neck, the deadly swellings stood out as white lumps. Bylot squeezed her limp hand but detected no response.

"I'm sorry," he choked out. "Can you forgive me?"

Evelyn's eyelids flickered open. For a moment Bylot recognized his beautiful sister of but a few days before. Then a spasm wracked her body, her back arched, her mouth opened in a silent scream and a trickle of black vomit and blood rolled down her chin.

Bylot knew this was her final pain even before the spasm relaxed. The open eyes he had looked into had not been focused on this world. As Evelyn's body sagged back onto the pillows, a calmness overcame her features. Gently he closed her eyes and mopped her brow. His tears spotted the quilted coverlet of his sister's deathbed.

"Forgive me," he mumbled. "I never insisted we leave. I was content to let the decision rest with you. I was weak."

Bylot was swamped by utter hopelessness. "Why must everything I touch be lost?" he asked the silent body. "My mother, my father, you. I could not even hold Dee and his library. I wished for a life of adventure and excitement, but what is that worth? Nothing. All I have found is death and loneliness."

Bylot blinked against his tears. There was too much horror in his life. What was the point of going on alone in this desolate world of suffering and pain?

"I shall not long outlast you," Bylot told Evelyn. Slowly and deliberately, he leaned forward and kissed her bloody lips. He tasted the bitterness of the diseased bile.

"A few days pain and we shall be together again," he said drawing back.

It was nearly dark now and the bell of the first dead-cart of the night rang its miserable request along the street. Bylot looked to the window, startled by the sound. "I cannot give you a peaceful tomb, but I shall not let them take you naked and anonymous in their damned carts."

Over the next hours, Bylot worked hard. With great care, he washed Evelyn's body, dressed her in her finest nightdress and wrapped her tightly in the sheets from the bed. For a small consideration, he rented a hand-drawn produce cart from the idle butcher on his street and, with considerable difficulty, half-carried, half-dragged Evelyn's body down the stairs into the street. A lantern hung from a pole at the front of the cart and, as Bylot worked, its light sent his wildly dancing shadow up and down the walls on either side of him. At last he was done and he stopped to regain his breath.

Bylot's options were few. He could not hope to pull the handcart far over the rough cobbles, especially at night. The closest churchyard was St. Barnabas, but the burial ground there was long full and had been closed. His best chance was the yard at the old nunnery of St. Stephens. It was farther, but he had heard tell that the carts from this area headed there. Taking a long breath, he hoisted the handles beneath his armpits and set off.

The journey was a nightmare of ι     dea
smells. Some shadowy figures stumblec     of
proach. Others lay still in the gutters. Scr     le
echoed from the surrounding buildings,     s
odour of death and decomposition hung ov
Bylot ignored it all. He had one thing left to
and he concentrated only on the next step that
him and his tragic burden closer to his goal.

At last he reached St. Stephens. Within the
wall of the burial ground, a pit that encompassed
the yard had been dug. It was near 40 feet in length, ς
wide and 20 deep. Flaming torches were set about the
to illuminate the work of the buriers, yet their effect ι
ly deepened the darkness instead of dispelling it. Hunc
figures moved hither and thither pursuing unmentiona
tasks, and the smell of death hung so strongly in the still a
that Bylot could barely breathe. It was a scene from hell made
real and played out but a half mile from Bylot's home.

None except the buriers and the dead-cart drivers were
allowed within the gate, and the yard was watched by a
custodian. Bylot recognized the man. He was an old sailor
for whom Bylot occasionally bought drinks in exchange for
the man's wondrous tales of the sea. "Aye, Master Bylot. 'Tis
an ill time 'n no mistakin'."

"Tom, I have come to bury my sister," Bylot said without
preliminaries.

"Ah. I be grieved for yer loss, but 'taint 'lowed."

"But Tom, would you have me throw her on a dead-cart?
Even in the worst storms at sea, you laid your own to rest."

"Aye, we did that." Tom hesitated. At that moment a

-cart rumbled up and Tom waved it through. The back
ιe cart was piled high with some fifteen or sixteen life-
remains, mostly in rags or naked. Tom regarded the
nging, skeletal limbs hanging over the back. "Go on," he
ı to Bylot, "but ye be quick if ye wish to remain so."

Bylot nodded and stumbled through the gate into hell.
ιe cart in front of him pulled to the very edge of the fear-
ιme pit, and the buriers unloaded it by simply tipping the
ι.arness. The cadavers, with loose limbs flapping all ways,
slid into the depths. The buriers immediately set about covering the load with earth.

It took all Bylot's courage to approach the pit. Dazed by
the horror surrounding him and exhausted by his journey,
Bylot struggled to unload the shroud-wrapped body from
the back of his cart. One of the buriers, seeing his difficulty,
put down his shovel and went over to help. Together they
carried Evelyn to the lip and, as gently as possible, placed
her in the hole. Bylot muttered a few words as his sister slid
into the depths. For a moment he was overwhelmed by a
desire to follow her, but the glimpse he caught of her final
resting place, distorted as it was through his tears, thrust
him almost physically back from the edge. Staggering
away, and mumbling incoherent prayers like a madman,
Bylot stumbled past the cart and out the gate into the wel-
coming blackness.

The rest of that night was a blur against which images
of unspeakable horror stood out with unnatural bright-
ness, like stars in a cloudless sky. In the hopeless darkness
of an alley, Bylot stumbled and fell into a pile of rags only
to find that he embraced the body of a man already begin-

ning to rot. Beneath the lantern above a tavern, he espied a young woman of some beauty sitting against the wall. On approach he noticed that her eyes were open, but that their gaze was fixed upon the eternity for which he was yearning. From within the tavern came the wild laughter and shouting of madmen facing death. Once, resting his aching bones against the wall of a house, he was overwhelmed by a scream so hideous that, as it rose in pitch, his blood chilled within his body. The sound stretched almost unbearably toward infinity before subsiding into the sobbing words, "My son. My son." Bylot fled. Eventually, overcome by exhaustion, he fell into a ditch and slept.

After what seemed but a few minutes, the pale sun woke Bylot and he rose, aching and half-dead, and began a stumbling walk into the city. He had no destination in mind other than to join Evelyn and it didn't matter where that happened. The narrow streets were almost empty and what figures Bylot did encounter shuffled away as quickly as possible. Houses on both sides were boarded up and watchmen stood at the corners.

Soon Bylot could drag his aching limbs no farther and he stood in the centre of the street, content to await whatever fate was planned for him. It was not what he expected or craved. In his desperation, Bylot was found by a tallow chandler, James Foe, who was returning from some meagre business. Foe recognized Bylot from some dealings in the past and stopped to render assistance.

"Where be ye headed?" Foe asked. All Bylot could manage was a half-hearted shrug.

"Well," Foe continued. "I be journeying by the river to

Mortlake and ye be welcome to join me if ye so wish."

The name Mortlake rang a bell deep in Bylot's overwhelmed mind. He nodded and Foe helped him mount the cart. He sat there quietly, oblivious to the journey. Eventually, the cart stopped.

"We be arrived," Foe informed his passenger. "I know not where ye wish to be, so I have brought ye to my destination."

"I wish to be dead," Bylot mumbled.

"And so ye shall be, as shall we all. But it will be in the Lord's good time."

With an extraordinary effort of will, Bylot roused himself and looked around. The cart stood in the forecourt of a large house. It had once been grand, but signs of age and neglect were everywhere. Some windows were broken and others covered with the ivy that straggled over the walls in profusion. Weeds poke up through the stone of the path leading to the front door.

As Bylot gazed listlessly on the scene, the door opened and a figure emerged. Even in his weary, self-absorbed state, Bylot recognized the man—his sharp, ancient features and long black cloak were unmistakable.

"Dee!" Bylot exclaimed.

"Aye," Foe answered. "'Tis John Dee himself that I make my delivery to. Are ye acquainted with the Magus?"

"He is, indeed," Dee said as he strode, smiling, to the side of the cart. "Master Bylot and myself are old friends, and I thank you for bringing him here. Welcome home, Robert."

# 6

## CIPHERS

For days Bylot lay abed in Dee's house at Mortlake, waiting for death to claim him. His basic needs were attended to by Dee's servants and, in time, with the dawning realization that death was ignoring him, Bylot returned, at least partway, to the living.

One day, Dee appeared at Bylot's bedside. "So, my young friend, you have returned."

"It was where the chandler brought me," Bylot replied, listlessly.

"Nothing happens without a purpose. Fate drew you back to my doorstep to continue your studies."

"What's the point?"

"You wish to die?" Dee asked.

Bylot shrugged, less certain now than he had been at Evelyn's deathbed.

"It is not your time, Robert Bylot. You have survived the pestilence and come as close as any man to death. Do you not see that you are destined?"

"For what?"

It was Dee's turn to shrug. "Who can say with certainty what role is written for us? All we can do is try to understand what the spirits tell us. They are telling you it is not time for death."

"Perhaps."

"Splendid. Then I shall expect you in the library tomorrow to continue your interrupted lessons."

Before Bylot could say anything else, Dee was gone.

Ψ

At first Bylot resisted Dee's pressure to learn, but with no alternatives, he began to fall back into his old patterns. At first he could not concentrate and found what lessons he attended frivolous, but time healed him and gradually the knowledge he was being offered brought him back to life. He even rationalized that he had a duty to continue learning for Evelyn's sake. As the months passed, his old excitement for his studies returned.

One day, four months after Bylot's arrival at Mortlake, Dee presented him with two volumes of a book to read, with instructions to pay particular care to its contents. Bylot sat for many nights by a candle, trying to absorb the mysterious text of *Steganographia*, written generations before by a German Benedictine Abbot, Johannes Trithemius. Page after page listed the names of angels and spirits through which adepts could transmit information in secret over great distances. Much was written in languages completely unintelligible to Bylot. What he could decipher talked of spells to summon the message-carrying spirits and the great complexities involved in summoning the right spirit. Apparently, bringing the wrong one, or one from too far away, could be extremely dangerous.

Bylot studied hard, but was loathe to approach Dee for

help and reveal his woeful ignorance. At length, one cold afternoon in October, Dee summoned Bylot to his workshop.

Such a summons was unusual, and Bylot never ceased to be fascinated by the room. The workshop at Mortlake was different from the undercroft at Clerkenwell. It was more of a laboratory and less of a library, although a number of books and manuscripts were scattered on shelves and window seats. Herbs and various dried plants hung from ceiling hooks, giving the room a sweet, aromatic smell, and the walls were lined with shelves of bottles containing all manner of strange liquids, both coloured and colourless. In some floated the pale, wrinkled bodies of animals—lizards, snakes and assorted sea creatures. On a large table in the centre of the room lay a collection of beakers and vials connected by glass tubes. On occasion, Bylot had seen some of the containers bubbling and coloured liquids dripping from the pipes. At these times, a much sharper odour permeated the air, catching at the back of Bylot's throat. Today, however, all was quiet.

"How do you progress with your task, young Bylot?" Dee asked as his apprentice entered the room.

Bylot stalled and talked of the angels and spirits he had come across, painfully aware that he understood little of the deeper meaning.

"You but scratch the surface of the surface," Dee interrupted. "Are you familiar with the Kabbalah?"

"A little. Do the Kabbalists not seek the word that the apostle John proclaimed was the beginning?"

"Indeed they do, but more. They also seek the true name of God and all his angels—some 301,655,172 by some calculations. They believe the names to be discernible through a study of numerology and the Hebrew alphabet. The Hebrew language is divided into three parts of speech that conform to the three levels of the universe: the divine, where the nine orders of angels live; the celestial, of the nine spheres of planets and stars; and the earthly, of the four prime elements. Look here how they are represented on this miniature alchemist's globe."

Dee picked up a small glass globe and handed it to Bylot. The outer surface was carved with nine winged figures—the angels inhabiting the divine level of creation, Bylot assumed. Inside and separated from the outer globe by a colourless liquid, was a smaller globe. On it Bylot could see inscribed the nine planets and stars of the celestial level. Below this and surrounded by a pale red liquid, lay a third, yet smaller globe. Patterns that looked vaguely familiar to Bylot were etched upon it but they were too small to see clearly. The third globe was divided into quarters containing, respectively, a black powder, a clear liquid, a grey dust and, in the final section, nothing visible. Each globe was held in place by a narrow glass neck that ran from the outside to the centre, and the contents of each were prevented from mixing by a thin glass stopper.

"You hold the universe in your hand," Dee said. "Spheres within spheres. Our mortal realm at the centre containing the four prime elements—fire, earth, water and air—aqua fortis around that, and at the top, the realm of the gods, aqua vitae to make us feel like gods."

As Bylot peered at the wonderfully etched object, turning it about, it slipped from his grasp and fell toward the floor. With remarkable speed, Dee shot out a hand, catching the globe before it had fallen a foot.

"Have a care," Dee said as he replaced the globe on a shelf. "There are powers here that you cannot guess at. Had this shattered on the floor and the contents mixed, we would both, at this moment, be dying a most horrible death."

"I'm sorry. It slipped," Bylot stammered inadequately.

"No matter." Dee brushed off his apology with a wave of his hand. "Consider the numbers—nine orders of angels, nine celestial spheres, four prime elements—nine added to nine added to four produces twenty-two, the number of letters in the Hebrew alphabet."

"So, in the *Steganographia*, the numbers of the angels Trithemius talks of is important?" Bylot asked, hopefully.

"Yes, but did you understand what Trithemius was saying?"

"No," Bylot admitted.

"That is because the *Steganographia* makes no sense on the surface. The message is beneath. What did you make of the incantations to summon the spirits?"

"I could make nothing of them. They are in a language of which I am not familiar."

"Of which no one is familiar." Dee seemed to be enjoying the cryptic nature of the conversation. "The language is of Trithemius's own devising, but to those who have the key, it can be rendered into intelligible Latin."

"The key?"

"Indeed, and this is where I have played you short. I gave you only the message, not the means to read it. You are an intelligent man, Bylot, and as well versed in the mathematical arts as any. If you could not decipher the code without the key, then few could."

"What does it really say, then?" Bylot asked, ignoring the compliment.

Dee reached for one of the volumes and opened it at a well-thumbed page. "Here is the beginning of the incantation to summon the angel Uriel: *Anue dorm eflupna porte relsatteun plyda struari.*"

Bylot looked helplessly at the gibberish on the page. "Some words look as if they might be of vulgar Latin origin, but I can make no sense of it."

"Until I tell you this—take each alternate letter of each alternate word and what do you see?"

Bylot gazed at the phrase anew—A**nu**e dorm e**flu**pna porte re**lsa**tte**un** plyda s**tru**ari. "Nefunestentur. Not defiled?"

"Yes, from Paul's injunction to not defile cities by burying bodies within their walls."

"So it is a book of code?"

"Exactly. One I discovered in Amsterdam many years past. The *Steganographia* was of great use to Walsingham and his spies in their pursuit of the late queen's enemies. I copied three volumes in but three days."

"But you gave me only two to study. The third is the key?"

"Yes."

"So," Bylot progressed slowly, trying to put it all together in his mind, "if you use the key to translate the *Steganographia*'s code, you get another book, a different one—a deeper layer beneath the surface?"

"One of them."

"One of them?" Bylot asked hopelessly. Just when he though he was beginning to understand, Dee told him there was more. "There are other layers of code?"

"There are always other layers beneath what we see or think we see. Until we become God and see perfectly, there will always be deeper layers to discover. The first translation—the one I did—gives verses and phrases from the bible in Latin. It proves the code, but the verses mean nothing on their own."

Bylot sighed. How would they ever get deep enough to discover something understandable?

Dee went on. "There is, however, a numeric code in the key volume. For years I struggled to apply it to the *Steganographia*, but got nowhere. I should have seen it, though! The numeric code doesn't apply to Trithemius's book, but to the biblical quotations that come out of the first translation. The numeric code does not apply to *Anue dorm eflupna porte relsatteun plyda struari* but to *Ne funestentur*."

Bylot was beginning to understand. It was a two stage process. The gibberish incantations in the *Steganographia* had to be translated into the Latin biblical quotes using only each alternate letter of each alternate word. Once that was done, the numeric code could be applied. Bylot felt excitement rising. He was getting close to something. "What is the key?"

Dee laughed. "So you become interested now. Well, look." Dee took up a quill and wrote NEFUNESTENTUR on a blank page. Below, he scratched $1_2 2_2 1_5$. "This is the key for that phrase. The main numbers are the letters to be kept. The subscript indicates how many are to be discarded. Thus, with NEFUNESTENTUR we keep the first letter, N.

Then we discard the next 2, E and F. We keep U and N and discard two more, E and S. Finally, we keep T and discard the final five, ENTU and R. What does that leave us with?"

"Nunt—the root of the verb tell."

"Exactly. With the number key a new story is told."

"And what does that story say?"

"What is worth attaining is worth a struggle." Dee produced a small package of bound papers from his cloak. "This is the key to both volumes. Now you can read them."

With that, Dee left. Intrigued, Bylot set to work immediately. The task was immense and took him almost a week in which he rarely slept. At the end, however, he had a story—although it was one he was not sure he understood. The night after he finished, Dee visited his room.

"So you are done," the old man said. "What do you make of the story?"

"It tells of the four prime elements—earth, air, fire and water. Much talks of how the elements combine to form all we know and how their proportions in or out of balance determine our humours and moods, and the state of the physical world about. This is common knowledge to all who seek to understand the world, but Trithemius goes further and relates the elements to locations on our earthly sphere. He even gives the locations by longitude and latitude."

"Indeed." Dee's eyes took on a gleam of excitement. "These are points where the earthly sphere comes into contact with the higher. They are points of great power where we may learn of many wonders. Certain rites carried out in the presence of material from these sacred sites can open to us the wonders of the Gods. If I can collect materials from these four prime points, I will have the tools to undertake the rites that will recreate the Golden Age of Troy, and bring a new dawn to our sadly decadent times."

"Have you collected the materials?"

"Unfortunately, no. But the pursuit of this knowledge has consumed much of my energies these last years, and I have made progress. Now, what else could you discern from your translations?"

"Earth is close by here, in London. Air is in the Polish city of Krakow. Fire is a mountain in Cathay. Water seems to be far to the west, in the new world. Do these places really offer us a glimpse of the divine sphere of angels?"

"Yes!" Dee exclaimed. "I have heard as much from the angels Uriel and Gabriel through my Crystallomancy with Skryers."

"Skryers? What are Skryers?"

"Not what but who. Skryers are those mortals who have been blessed with a special gift. Their souls are in tune with the upper spheres. Thus they can be used to channel energy from the angels themselves down to our world. But we are not at that stage yet. I have visited only two of these places, although I can confirm their extraordinary power."

"Which two?"

"The first you, too, have visited—it is the site of my house in Clerkenwell. It is the location of the prime element earth, and there I conducted experiments in many of the scientific and conjuring arts. The contacts with angels was stronger there than anywhere. The site has an aura of quite remarkable power."

"Do you think the Romans sensed the power and built there deliberately?" Bylot asked.

"An interesting idea. I do not think that the Romans in general were particularly sensitive to the power of the other worlds, but individuals may well have been. In any case, what is certain is that Brutus and the descendants of the Trojans felt it. Why else would they have established themselves at London?"

"So, the Trojans knew of all four powerful locations?"

"Of course. The points were key to the Golden Age and if they preserved any knowledge when Troy fell, it would have been those four locations. If not, how could they possibly recapture the glorious past? I believe that, over generations, the Trojans attempted to reclaim the four points. They sent expeditions out. Brutus we know of, but the others ..."

As Dee's voice trailed off, Bylot imagined the desperate Trojans, assailed on all sides by people they considered barbarians, sending out parties of adventurers with vital pieces of ancient knowledge. How they fell into despair as, time after time, their expeditions disappeared into the unknown.

"Unfortunately," Dee began again, "the aura is not only discernible to adepts. If it is strong enough, it can sometimes have an effect on the common rabble as well. To them it is but an unknown feeling that can instill only fear and hatred. These were the emotions that led to the destruction of my house, workshop and library.

"But no matter. Before the disaster, I dug a sack of earth from beneath the undercroft and I keep it even now in my private study."

"It's not necessary to conduct the rites at one of the prime sites?"

"No. It would be beneficial and, I suspect, the ideal would be to conduct four rites simultaneously at the four sites, but that is not possible with our debased wisdom.

"Anyway, I have the sample of earth and, even as my possessions were consumed by fire, I was departing to seek air amidst a swirling whirlwind on the borders of Muscovy.

"Krakow is a primitive city compared to our own fair London, but the power there is palpable. The place is well known for atmospheric disturbances such as the whirlwinds I experienced there, and many local legends talk of airborne ships and diverse creatures flying through the night. To my sacred earth, I have added a large flask of air from a whirlwind."

Bylot was fascinated despite himself—lost civilizations, Golden Ages, magic locations, secret codes—it was all wonderful. "And of the other two prime locations?" he asked eagerly.

"The other two are more difficult as they do not lie in civilized parts of the world. I had high hopes of several expeditions, both to Cathay and the New World, but none have succeeded. I am too old now and doubt if I will see the completion of the task. But a younger man might."

A thrill passed through Bylot, but Dee continued without giving him a chance to grasp the full meaning.

"The fire of Cathay should be easy to attain. The peoples thereabouts have a measure of civilization and will be subject to the aura. This will lead a determined explorer to the correct spot.

"That is why I am scheming to create an expedition to the Spiceries to rival the commercial ventures of the short-sighted Smythe and the others. This new King James is not as fixed on the monopoly of trade as the late Queen and, I am sure, will allow my scheme to bear fruit. Will you be a part of it?"

Bylot hesitated in some confusion, thoughts swirling in his head like the whirlwind of Dee's tale. What was he being offered? Not command of a full voyage—no one would countenance such inexperience in such a high place, and surely not the continuance of Dee's life's work.

"You hesitate." Dee smiled. "That is natural. You do not know what I offer and it is good to be cautious. Let me enlighten you.

"Do you remember seeing Lancaster and Davis off these three years past?"

"Vividly. And his five ships' return laden with spices a year ago. They also, I believe, left some eight sailors, three factors and a pinnace as the foundation for a trading colony at Bantam."

"Aye," Dee said with a laugh. "It was an event I cursed as enriching Smythe. Everywhere they overmatched the Portuguese carracks, but the gods smiled. When Lancaster returned, above 38,000 were already dead of the plague in London. The pits were full and the docks silent. Do you recall Thomas Dekker's doggerel?

"No Music now is heard but bells.
And all their tunes are sick men's knells;
And every stroke the bell does toll,
Up to heaven it winds a soul."

Mention of the plague and the pits brought hideous memories flooding back to Bylot. It was all he could do to force them down and suppress his tears.

"I remember," he managed to croak out.

"Excellent. There were no cheering crowds to welcome Lancaster and Davis back, only empty, echoing wharves and the rumble of the dead-carts. But that was of little trouble. Half Lancaster's own men were dead, and the city merely suffered what he and his crew had experienced the past thirty months. Only one death troubled Lancaster—that of the good queen some months before the *Red Dragon*'s return.

"King James is a coarse and haughty Scot who understands nothing of the subtleties of his predecessor's policy. Even better, shortly before Lancaster's return, the King had been presented with a large quantity of peppers plundered from a Portuguese vessel. He insisted upon selling his loot before Lancaster could market his. Deep in debt, Smythe and the others pushed for an immediate return with another expedition. Lancaster refused to go so soon, and Davis was scapegoated for being wrong about the low cost of spices at Bantam, so command was given to one of Lancaster's lieutenants, Henry Middleton. He sailed almost immediately back to Bantam.

"This could not be better for my purposes. Smythe is distracted with this new venture and Davis is available for our voyage and willing to go. Furthermore, the King already has a commander in mind for the voyage, Sir Edward Michelborne. Michelborne is a useless fop to be sure, but with Davis and you beneath him, he will serve our purposes well enough. What do you say?"

Bylot's hesitance had passed. As Dee had spoken, he had seen opportunities for adventure and advancement blossom before him. This was the chance he had sought, and the revival of his painful memories of Evelyn's death only cemented the idea that he would do best to leave the city altogether.

"I will go," he said.

"Splendid. Then we must undertake our preparations with all haste."

# 7

## Fire

Michelborne, with John Davis as chief pilot, set sail in two ships, the *Tyger* and *Tyger's Whelp*, on December 5, 1604. Bylot sailed as Davis's apprentice and spent the first weeks of the voyage in a lather of excitement at the novelty around him. In his spare moments, he watched the crew crawl up the rigging, furl and unfurl the sails, and carry out the hundred tasks that kept the vessel running and on course. He loved the smell of tar and scrubbed wood, and lay awake at night, swinging gently in his hammock, listening to the ship's timbers creak and groan like a living creature. Even the first storm they encountered was a thrill once he got over the feeling that the ship was about to plunge into the next wave and sink to the bottom of the sea.

Davis seemed happy to take Bylot under his wing and was perfectly content to spend his spare time on the long, monotonous voyage around Cape Horn and across the Indian Ocean helping the younger man refine his navigational skills.

Davis was a rugged man, past middle age, but still strong. His blue eyes glinted with youthful humour, even though his face was scarred and wrinkled from a lifetime facing into ocean gales. Unlike Michelborne, who wore the finest clothes, Davis favoured a sailor's plain leather jerkin and loose leggings tucked into high boots.

Bylot liked Davis immediately and thoroughly enjoyed his tales of Drake, the Gilberts and Sir Walter Raleigh. Bylot listened to the soft west-country accent and absorbed as much as he could. At times, after Davis had told a particularly interesting tale, Bylot wondered if this was how Evelyn had felt when he related the things he had learned at school.

"If you wish to be a voyager on undiscovered seas," Davis was fond of saying, "you must know much more than navigation. You must know how to handle men, and not commonly the best sort, when they are suffering mightily from hunger, cold, illness and a perfectly natural fear of the unknown."

Davis's stories of his three voyages in search of the Northwest Passage rekindled the childhood excitement Bylot had felt when secretly discussing pirates and buccaneers with his sister. He paid particular attention when Davis talked of his third voyage—the one on which he discovered the Furious Overfall that Dee was convinced led into the fabled Straits of Anian.

"In the summer of 1587 we explored as far as 72 degrees 46 minutes north, beyond the reach of any other navigator," Davis said proudly one warm, clear night as the pair stood on the quarterdeck. The sea was as calm as glass and a long, greenish, phosphorescent wake glimmered behind them.

"The ice forced us back, of course. It always did, but we discovered a wondrous place as we returned. I was resting below when I noticed the ship rolling and pitching most unnaturally. I was about to investigate when I was called by the mate, one Henry Hudson." Davis looked distracted for a moment. "Perhaps you know of the Hudsons? They are from your part of England."

Bylot shook his head.

"No matter," Davis went on. "Thomas Hudson is an important man in the city, but Henry is a sailor much after my own heart. He was about your age when we sailed together. I shall introduce you to him when we return.

"After I went on deck with Hudson, I noticed that, although there was no wind or storm, there was a strong tide running from the west. The sea was extremely choppy and confused, and several plates of ice were being swept along at a considerable pace. It was obvious to me that this tide must emanate from some as yet undiscovered inlet.

"For several hours we tacked and beat our way against the current. We made progress, but conditions became steadily more dangerous for our small vessel. At length we approached a deep fold in the surface of the sea into which the tide raced with furious speed. Whirlpools of a size that would have frozen even Odysseus's heart spun about, and vast mountains and bergs of ice crashed together with a frightful grinding noise."

Davis fell silent, reliving the moment in his mind's eye.

"The Furious Overfall?" Bylot asked.

"I see you have heard of it." Davis smiled at his memories. "I came within an ace of ordering the ship into it."

"Why did you not?"

"Oh, we should have been crushed for certain. No ship of our size could withstand the force of that tide or of those icebergs. But I was convinced I was seeing the Northwest Passage to Cathay and I swore I would return to attempt it the following year."

"But you did not."

"No, I did not. Instead I went to war."

"The Armada?"

Davis nodded. "I had no choice. None of us did. Every man and ship was needed if the Spanish king were not to succeed."

"But you did not return the year after, either, when the Armada had been defeated."

Davis looked hard at Bylot. "You are young yet and have much to see and experience. I saw something that summer of 1588 that spoiled me for the sea for many a year."

Bylot waited patiently, while Davis drifted off into his memories.

Eventually, he continued. "I was captain of the *Black Dog*, a small vessel used mostly for ferrying supplies as we hounded the Spanish fleet along the channel. But after the fire ships went in off Calais, we went for what plunder we could find. We found and overtook a crippled galleass."

"Galleass?" Bylot had never heard the term.

"Vessels specially built with both oar and sail for work in all conditions. They were heavily armed, having upward of forty brass cannon each, but they had one fatal weakness—rows of unprotected rowers on their decks.

"At first we were elated at taking such a prize, even though we were not responsible for its disablement. This would also be our first chance in a long, tiring week to catch a close sight of our enemy. The vessel looked to be sound although she drifted helplessly. Her oars were shattered, her rigging and sails torn, and her masts splintered.

"As the *Black Dog* drew alongside, I, cutlass in hand, was one of the first on board. The decking of the Spaniard was not complete over the heads of the rowers, only enough to hold a few of the ship's cannon that now lay at all angles. The upper deck was near deserted with the exception of a few corpses and a cluster of obviously helpless men at the far end. I determined to go below and see what I could find there. I have ever since wished that I had not."

Davis paused again and it was all Bylot could do to hold his tongue. But he had to. The story would only come out in Davis's own time.

Davis looked sombre as he continued. "Grasping my cutlass before me, I descended to the lower levels. At first I could see little, there being such a contrast between the background gloom and the bright shafts of sunlight that cut through the numerous ragged holes in the vessel's sides. The air was fetid and sweet smelling, and I was surrounded by groans and cries in a variety of languages. At first I thought I had landed in some infirmary but as my eyes adjusted, I began to see a sight infinitely worse than any plague hospital.

"I stood on a centre deck, the surface of which was slick with blood. On either side, the deck was set down a foot or two, and benches held the rowers. There were four rowers to each oar, or there had been. Most were dead, cut about by the shot that had traversed the length of the ship. Some bodies were complete, but many were most horribly mutilated. Severed limbs lay about, some still chained to seats. Shattered torsos spilled their secrets all ways and grotesque heads leered at me from every side. Between the horrors, several inches of what I at first took to be water lapped the seats and bodies. The realization that it was blood and the surge in my stomach happened simultaneously. I fell to my knees and retched uncontrollably.

"When I was done, I became aware of a voice close by my ear. 'Be ye English?' it asked.

"'Aye,' I stammered, looking around. The voice came from a man sitting at the oars. I could see his upper body above the lip of the deck. He was ragged and filthy, and I judged him to be of middle age.

"'Be we victorious?'

"'Aye. It seems so. The Spaniard runs before us now.'

"'Then England be safe?'

"'For now, I think so.'

"The man sighed contentedly. 'That be good. It has been twenty years since I have been in the company of stout Englishmen.'

"'Why?'

"'I was captured at Hawkins's battle of San Juan de Ulloa where we were so treacherously betrayed. Ten of us were held captive, tortured by the Inquisition and sent to the galleys. Now I shall die a free man.'

"'Then let me unchain you,' I said rising slightly.

"'No,' the man said. 'There be no need. I have but one favour to ask of thee.'

"'Ask away.'

"'Be that cutlass sharp?'

"'Aye.'

"'Then take it if ye own pity in thy heart and with a single blow end my suffering.'"

Davis gazed over the ship's rail at the dark sea. "I asked the man why and offered him the surgeons aboard our ships. He man laughed bitterly. 'Surgeons be but butchers and they be no use to me now unless they wield a cutlass better than thee.'

"As he talked, I pulled myself up. When I was near standing, I could see down into the blood-soaked pit in which the man lay. A ball had come through the side of the vessel beside him. It had killed his companions, whose remains lay around him, but it had not killed him—yet. Below the man's waist was nothing recognizable as human.

"'Ye see. I have no need of a surgeon. Now, the cutlass.'

"I stood rigid for an age, gazing down at the horror and the man's imploring eyes. I had seen my share of dead men in my travels, but the horrors of that hold and of this man's pitiful remains I hope never to see again.

"But I had no choice. In what seemed like slow motion, I raised my weapon. At its height I hesitated again. The man smiled at me and nodded gently. I closed my eyes and brought the cutlass down. I felt it slice through flesh and bone and I heard the man sigh, but I saw nothing, my eyes were closed. Dropping the cutlass and impervious to the piteous cries around me, I fled back onto the upper deck.

"Never had sunlight seemed so clean and pure as it did upon my escape from that hellish hold. It took some hours for my hands to cease their shaking and for my stomach to settle, but I swore to myself in that first instant that as long as I lived and as long as it were in my power, I should never partake in war or put another man's life in danger.

"So, you see, young Bylot. 'Tis not all adventure and excitement in the seafaring life. There is horror aplenty in the doings of men."

Bylot stood silent, imagining the horrors Davis had seen. It was a war long ago and Bylot had no intention of fighting in sea battles; still, the images of the mutilated rowers and the dying man pleading for an end haunted him.

"That day nearly finished me," Davis went on. "Even in the excitement of our great victory over the Spanish, I could not forget the rower I killed. Every time I closed my eyes for rest, his smiling face swam into view. It nearly drove me to madness. Naught seemed to matter but man's inhumanity to man. I forgot the Overfall and swore I would never go to sea again. I went to the land in my native Dorset and occupied myself with the family farm."

"Yet, here you are."

"Indeed," Davis took a deep breath and turned to Bylot. "I am not a farmer," he said with a smile. "After a few years, I found myself talking with the pigs of the Northwest Passage and the Furious Overfall. I described icebergs and Esquimaux to squabbling chickens. I knew the sea was my life. But more than that, it was my master."

Davis's smile faded and he stared at Bylot seriously. "Be careful, young Bylot, of your dreams of exploration. Once begun, searching cannot easily be put aside. I had everything a man could want on my farm, a loving wife, gainful employment and five healthy children. Many a man would kill for what I had. Yet I was dissatisfied. A demon had been born when I first spied those churning waters. It nagged me and would allow no rest. I had to return."

"But you never went back to the Furious Overfall?"

"I have not yet had the chance, Thomas Smythe has sent me here."

"I know Smythe."

"Many do," Davis replied, "and many come to regret it. He is a powerful man, and like all powerful men is concerned only with his own affairs. Be wary of Smythe if you cross him again. He will use you and discard you at his whim.

"Nonetheless, he has promised a voyage to the Furious Overfall after my return with Michelborne."

"I shall come with you!" Bylot exclaimed impulsively. "If you will have me."

Davis laughed out loud. "You remind me much of myself at your age, Robert. I will have you gladly. Your youth and enthusiasm shall pull this old man through his mad ventures. Perhaps together we shall sail the Straits of Anian and find a shorter, English, route to Cathay."

Bylot retired to his hammock and lay, listening to the groans of the ship and snores of the other sailors, his mind alive with possibilities. But first he had to discover Dee's fire rock. He fell asleep, hoping its location would not be too difficult to find.

Ψ

Bylot need not have worried. The instant Bantam was sighted, the fire rock's location became obvious. In the gathering dusk as they lay offshore, the entire island of Gunung Api appeared to be ablaze.

Michelborne's main preoccupation upon reaching Bantam appeared to be plunder, and he busied himself attacking any and every ship he came across, regardless of origin. Bylot worried increasingly as the time for departure home neared. Eventually, in desperation, he confided his purpose in Davis. "I must get to that island."

"Why?" Davis asked. "There's nothing there but barren rock."

"I must collect a piece of that rock. It is something I promised to do for Dr. Dee."

"So, you work for the Magus. There is more to you than meets the eye. Still, I will see what I can do."

The following day, Davis asked Bylot to join him on board the *Tyger's Whelp* and ordered the anchor raised.

"Where do we head?" Bylot asked.

"For your mystical rock," Davis responded, "although others think we seek new groves of nutmeg on the island of fire. I do not believe for a moment in Dee's magic, but you have committed to a task and must fulfill your duty."

The ship anchored in one of the few safe coves on the rugged shore of Gunung Api. Above the tiny vessel, the dark cone of the volcano loomed threateningly. Flames periodically leapt from the crater and illuminated the undersides of the clouds of black smoke that roiled over the summit. Rocks, some as large as houses, rumbled down the mountainside while smaller ones flew through the air and crashed into the sea around.

"I do not envy you your task," Davis mused as he gazed

at the fearful scene, "but I shall hold the *Whelp* here against your return as long as I am able. Be swift."

Bylot fought down a rising sense of dread as he waded ashore and stumbled up the steep, ash-covered slope. Was this indeed a magical place that might help resurrect a Golden Age for mankind? There was certainly a power to the island. As Bylot struggled up the slopes, he felt the mountain call to him. The call grew stronger with each step, overwhelming his fear of death and convincing him that Dee was right about this extraordinary place.

Bylot progressed upward, dividing his attention between keeping his footing and avoiding hot, flying rocks. He had almost given up searching for a sign to tell him what to collect when a great boulder, dislodged by a tremor, rolled from the lip of the crater toward him. Bylot barely had time to hurl himself aside as it crashed past. Terrified and determined to return to the ship regardless of the summons and Dee's instructions, Bylot hauled himself to his feet. It was then he saw it—a long, rope-like black rock. It was near a foot in length, pointed at either end and twisted oddly in the middle. It looked like soft mud squeezed out from under a shoe, yet it was as hard as iron. This must have been born in the deep heart of the volcano's fire. Surely there was no better sample for Dee.

Grabbing the rock, Bylot fled down the hillside. The activity behind him was increasing, almost, Bylot thought, as if the volcano was angry at his desecration. Bylot reached the boat as red-hot rocks crashed about and hissed into the waters of the bay. As he scrambled aboard, he was met by Davis, holding a pistol in each hand.

"They wished to leave you to the mountain," Davis said, waving a pistol at the crew who stood sullenly by the wheel, "and I must honestly say that I saw much merit in the idea. But I have grown fond of you, Robert Bylot, and I would miss our conversations if you were incinerated here. Did you find what you sought?"

"I did." Bylot proudly held up the rock.

"Good, then let us be on our way. Raise the anchor." The crew set to with a will and the ship was soon pulling away from the island.

Bylot was happy with the completion of his task and eager to return in triumph to Dee. But Michelborne had other ideas and intercepted a Japanese junk off the Malay coast in hopes of more plunder.

No sooner had the *Tyger* drawn alongside than a host of pirates—squat heavily armed men, with leathery, weather-beaten skin and narrow eyes—leapt on board. They were dressed in variously coloured robes held with cords, and their black hair was tied in topknots. Each waved a long, curved, two-handed sword. In the chaotic fighting that swept the decks, the crew became separated.

Bylot, Michelborne and most of the men found themselves huddled in the foredeck as frightful noises emanated from the cabins aft. All at once, a man burst through the door. His clothes were severely cut and numerous wounds gaped all about his body. A stream of startlingly bright blood pulsed from his neck between the fingers of his vainly clutching right hand.

He took two stumbling steps forward and attempted to speak, but no words came forth, only a fresh gout of blood.

Sinking to his knees, the man threw his arms out in hopeless supplication before pitching forward on his face. As he twitched and trembled, the blood formed a large pool by his head. Then he lay still. John Davis was dead.

As Bylot stared in horror, more than twenty of the pirates appeared through the door. Several had clumps of skin and hair hanging like trophies from their bloody swords.

"We are done!" Michelborne cried in despair.

Bylot could only agree. The Englishmen's short swords and daggers were no match for the long, narrow swords the pirates wielded. Backed into a corner, Bylot and the others could hope only to sell their lives as dearly as possible.

"The pikes!" A voice yelled from behind the terrified men.

Bylot turned to see a sailor standing by the hatch. He was holding one of the twelve-foot-long pikes that Michelborne had insisted on bringing, despite Davis's objections that they were a useless waste of space and weight. Now they might save their lives.

Frantically, the sailor hauled weapon after weapon from the hold below and passed them to his companions. Bylot's felt heavy and unwieldy.

The pirates had stopped beside Davis's body to watch the new development. As the surviving crew rushed forward with a maniacal yell, the pirates fled. Those too slow were impaled. Bylot pinned a man against the far bulkhead and left his body arching in agony.

About a dozen of the Japanese took refuge in the bowels of the ship where they could not be approached by more than two men at a time and where the long pikes were useless.

"Bring up the demi-culverins," Michelborne shouted.

Two of the thirty-two pound weapons were brought forward and loaded with musket balls, case-shot and chains. They were fired simultaneously through the cabin wall. Smoke, wood splinters and shrieks of agony filled the air, followed by a heavy silence.

Bylot was first to peer through the doorway. The carnage in the confined space turned his stomach. Every surface was smeared with blood and it was several inches deep on the floor. Severed limbs and unidentifiable pieces of flesh lay all around. Those still alive were horribly mutilated and groaned pitiably until sailors entered and ended their misery.

Bylot retreated onto the deck. The fresh air was welcome, but he was faced with John Davis's bloody body. All the satisfaction Bylot had felt at finding the fire rock had vanished. Instead, he found himself thinking of the Furious Overfall. John Davis would never make that voyage again. Bylot would have to find some other way.

# 8

## SKRYING

B ylot and the *Tyger* arrived back in England in the summer of 1606 with the news of Davis's death. As soon as the ship docked, Bylot hurried to Mortlake, eager to discharge his duty to Dee. He found the Magus in his public study, looking considerably older than he remembered.

"Ah, Bylot," Dee said, turning from his maps and charts. "I had almost given you up for dead."

"Not I," Bylot replied, "but John Davis's bones lie in Cathay waters."

"Did you get it?" Dee asked, ignoring the news of the explorer's death.

"Yes." Bylot removed the twisted piece of rock from his cloak and handed it to Dee.

"Excellent. Excellent. And this is from the fire?"

"From the very mouth of hell atop Gunung Api."

"Not hell, my friend. Heaven."

Clutching his new prize, Dee retreated through an oak door on the far side of the room into his private study. As he left he called ahead, "Henry, come and entertain young Bylot while I examine our prize."

Bylot was shocked to see the tall, thin form of Henry Greene appear from Dee's inner sanctum. The man had filled out a bit over the years, but his sharp nose and greenish-grey eyes were distinctive. He was well dressed, and his walk had a confident swagger that Bylot didn't remember.

"What are you doing here?" Bylot asked.

Greene ignored the question. Instead, his face broke into a smile. It was a formal expression, never touching the hard eyes that gazed stonily at Bylot. Greene stepped forward and offered his hand.

"It has been many a year, Robert," he said in a strangely soft voice, quite unlike the one Bylot remembered from St. Paul's great church. "The Magus has told me much about the services you perform for him."

Automatically, Bylot grasped the proffered hand. The grip was strong, but the flesh strangely cold. He repeated his question. "What are you doing here?"

"I have been here all along. Did you not think it strange that Dee approached you outside Founders Hall on the night Smythe rejected your appeal?"

All at once, that evening made sense.

"You took me there to meet Dee, not Smythe! You knew Smythe would turn me down."

Greene nodded slightly. "The ways of the Magus are varied."

Bylot didn't know what to think. He remembered his anger and embarrassment at being abandoned by Greene, but it had all been part of a plan. He had been manipulated shamelessly. "What do you do for Dee now?"

"I am his skryer."

Instinctively, Bylot withdrew his hand and stepped back. He remembered Dee telling him of these men—mediums between the world of man and the spirits, supposedly gifted with strange powers to see into and communicate with the higher spheres.

"My gifts unsettle you," Greene almost whispered.

"I have never met one of your kind."

"We are but ordinary men blessed with extraordinary talents that the Magus finds of use. We are to have an action this very eve. Perhaps you could join us?"

Bylot was about to make an excuse when Dee returned from the other room. "Indeed. You must. The fire is excellent. You must see Greene's talents and catch a glimpse of the world we seek."

Bylot hesitated. A part of him wanted to leave, yet he was being offered a chance to peer into a world of mystery that very few ever saw.

"What harm can it do?" Dee went on, sensing his uncertainty. "You will learn something. It will be my gift to you in recompense for obtaining the Fire."

Bylot's curiosity was getting the better of him. "Very well."

Greene's smile broadened. "Good. Then as soon as the sun's rays reach the window and illuminate the crystal, we shall begin. Shall we commence purification and prayers?"

"Yes. Yes," Dee said with more enthusiasm than Bylot had seen in the old man for years.

The next hour was spent in ritual purification. After assuring Dee and Greene that he had not engaged in any of the seven deadly sins over the past three days, Bylot bathed, shaved and trimmed his fingernails. Then, as he looked on, Dee and Greene chanted unintelligible invocations five times to each of the four cardinal points—north, south, east and west.

"Is the moon now in its firstmost quarter?" Greene asked.

"It is," Dee replied.

"And is Jupiter placed well in a Fire house?"

"It is."

"Then it is time."

Dee led the way through the heavy oak door into his private study. Bylot had never been allowed in before, and he looked about eagerly.

Around the walls a great assortment of shelves carried all manner of measuring instruments, variously coloured glass flasks of quite wonderful design, and books. A vast globe stood in one corner beneath an ornate hourglass. Beside it sat a large book chest, the carved lid secured with two heavy brass locks. A carpet of strange, eastern design covered the centre of the floor and on it sat a reading table, complete with an angled lectern and a loaded, revolving book store.

To Bylot's left, the wall was cut by the room's only window, a glowing sheet of latticed glass that stretched from the dark oak ceiling almost to the floor. A narrow ledge below the window was cluttered with curled manuscripts and more books, a second hourglass and a polished human skull. In front of the ledge sat a low, bare table. The top was square and its surface divided by engraved lines that formed a hexagram. Around the edges were letters of an alphabet Bylot had never seen. Squares of interlocking words in the same alphabet were placed around the table, the largest in the centre of the hexagram.

"My table of practice," Dee explained. "The alphabet is the Enochian, communicated to me by angels our friend Henry spoke with when we journeyed to Krakow."

Dee crossed to the book chest by the globe and unlocked it. With elaborate care, he lifted out a large crystal sphere. It appeared to be made of clear natural crystal, but Bylot noted that, toward the centre, it became strangely cloudy. Dee carefully placed the ball on top of the mysterious words at the centre of his table of practice. Greene sat cross-legged on the floor across the table from the window, Dee sat on the floor to his right, a notebook open beside him, and Bylot was ushered to Greene's left. The sun streamed through the west-facing window and played on the crystal sphere.

"One word of warning," Dee said. "Greene is most adept at summoning beneficial spirits, but evil lurks everywhere and conspires to trick us. Whatever you see or hear, do not intervene. Only a skryer may communicate with the spirits and the involvement of one who has not the power might greatly anger those whose beneficence we seek."

Bylot nodded.

"Further," Dee continued, "Greene will speak in both our language and that of the angels. It is of respect to them who understand everything."

Beside Bylot, Greene sat immobile, staring unblinkingly into the crystal. Nothing happened for what seemed like an age, and Bylot had trouble not fidgeting to ease the aches in his legs and back. The cross-hatched shadows of the window moved slowly across the table and, although he dared not look around, Bylot was aware of the shadows moving in the room around him. At the edge of his vision, he saw the round shadow of the globe lengthen and stretch along the wall. It was as if the hard reality of the room was wavering and becoming fluid.

At length, Greene sighed and Bylot sensed Dee tense across from him. Greene began a mumbled intonation in a language unfamiliar to Bylot. His voice, which before had been somewhat high pitched, had taken on a deep resonance that Bylot found strangely relaxing.

Bylot stared at the crystal as Greene's mesmerizing voice droned on. The shadows around him darkened and drew in until the only thing he could see was the crystal, almost painfully bright as it focused the evening sunlight. It was as if he were gazing down a long, dark tunnel and the lights and shadows wavered and swirled at the far end of it. The colours and configurations in the crystal's depths were beautiful. They seemed to form shapes and patterns but, concentrate as he might, Bylot could not recognize them. He felt he was on the edge of seeing something real, but at the instant he grasped it, it dissolved. The more he strained to see, the less sure he became of what he saw.

Eventually, Greene broke into archaic-sounding English. "I see thee. And I know thee. Thou art Uriel, who helped Michael to bury Adam."

Without removing his gaze from the crystal, Greene changed to his normal voice and addressed Dee. "It is Uriel for certain. He stands, dressed in resplendent robes as we saw him at the skrying in Krakow."

Dee wrote hurriedly in his journal. "Will he entertain a question?" he asked when he had finished.

"Aye." Greene returned to his spirit voice.

"Are you happy that we have attained the third element?" Dee asked.

"*Gothos azam cthola apnam baradat?*" Greene interpreted.

There was silence for a moment. Then Greene addressed Dee in the deep monotone. "The task has been long and nears fruition. One who was not here comes now to complete it. Then all mysteries shall be unearthed and the Age of Gold come to man."

Dee scribbled frantically. "Will we meet with success in our enterprise?"

"If water ye seek then water ye shall find in plenty. Water that shall tower above thee and hold thee fast to thy task," Greene intoned.

"Do we have the blessings of the angels for our task?"

There was a particularly long pause after Greene translated the question. Eventually, he said, "The angels look with pleasure upon all works that bring the divine light of the spheres to illuminate fallen man."

As the shadows moved and the light played on the crystal, Dee continued questioning Greene and Uriel. Some questions referred to the collection of the four elements, but others referred to things of which Bylot knew nothing— fires in the sky, new stars, the Fiery Trigon and various astrological signs. Bylot's eyes grew heavy with the effort of concentration and he felt his mind drift. Was Greene a charlatan or a genuine skryer? Bylot had no way of knowing. If only he could see something he could be sure of.

Gradually, Bylot became aware of a voice, different from Greene's or Dee's. It was light as gossamer and seemed to come to him from inside his head rather than through his ears.

"Look deep. Look deep," it said.

Confused, Bylot strained to make sense of the colours inside the crystal. His eyes burned and his head ached.

There was something! A small shape deep a swirl of red.

"Dost thou see me?" the voice asked.

"I don't know."

"Then look harder, for I am here and I see thee."

Bylot squinted painfully. The shape dissolved and then reappeared, larger and more solid. Could it be a figure? A small child? A girl?

Bylot's heart leaped—Evelyn?

Bright, tinkling laughter filled Bylot's head. "Nay, I be not your sister, though she be happy to be free of the mortal coil and awaits thee. Look deeper."

"I think I see."

"Thou canst skry a little, I warrant. What dost thou see?"

"A child," Bylot said uncertainly. "But not Evelyn."

The laughter returned, like precious gems rattling in a fine crystal glass. Bylot felt himself smile.

"A child of God, but not as ye know childhood. We were old before thy world was formed."

"What is your name?"

"I have many names. Those in this room knowest me as Madami."

"Where do you live?"

"Everywhere and nowhere." Again the tinkling laugh. "But this babble is of no consequence. I am but a child and must return, but I would tell thee things."

"What things?"

"What wouldst thou know?"

"I don't know. Everything."

"Ha. Thou presumes to seek the wisdom of God."

"No! I do not presume that."

"Then what would thou knowest? The secrets of the skies? The Philosopher's Stone?"

Bylot thought for a minute. "I do not wish the alchemical secrets. Those are for the likes of Dee. I wish simply to know the world on which we live—its oceans and continents, rivers and coasts, mountains and valleys. I wish to know what lies beyond Meta Incognita."

"Thou wishes to make the unknown known. That is a mighty task and not for one alone. Time changeth. All things come to their fullest in time. Yet some of the corners and straights of the world are for thee to see. The searching shall be hard and thy friends shall fall away. Those ye know shall die and ye be marked for loneliness. Thou shall succeed but be cursed with unrecognized greatness."

"Thou mayest question," Greene's deep spirit voice intruded into Bylot's reverie.

"What?" he asked as the tiny figure of Madami wavered and disappeared. Laughter echoed in his head, but whether it was of happiness or cruelty he could not tell.

"Uriel shall favour thee with an answer," Greene said.

Bylot's mind whirled. Another question. For another spirit. What should he ask? Did Greene know about his conversation with Madami? Dee's face swam into focus across the table. It seemed to hang suspended above the crystal that glowed with the final rays of the sun.

"What?" Bylot stuttered. "Will I find happiness on this earth?" he blurted out.

"Fool!" Greene thundered in his spirit voice. "The mysteries of the cosmos are open to thee. Thou could walk with Aristotle and Copernicus. And what dost thou seek? Petty happiness in thy mortal span."

"I'm sorry," Bylot cowered before the verbal onslaught.

"Nonetheless, I shall answer thee. Thou hast been and will be blessed and content twice, which is more than most of your mortal kin. The first was thine until the darkness of the pit overcame it. The second shall be when your dreams are answered by the earthly sphere."

A wave of dizziness swept over Bylot. When it passed, he felt incredibly tired. It was as if a huge weight had settled on his shoulders and was pressing him down into the floor. He looked around slowly. The room had returned to normal. The fading light reflected off a simple glass sphere on the table. No angels danced within it. Dee and Greene regarded Bylot curiously.

"Did you see her?" Bylot said slowly.

"Who?" Dee asked.

"Madami."

Dee and Greene exchanged glances. "What did she say?" Dee inquired.

"She laughed a lot and said I should be lonely and unrecognized. Did you not hear her?"

"You but mumbled unintelligibly," Greene said. "But that is the way of the spirits. Sometimes they do not wish others to hear what they say. You can skry some, Bylot."

"I'm tired."

"Of course." Dee stood. "You are welcome to stay. Your old room is free."

"Thank you." With some effort, Bylot struggled to his feet and stumbled out of the room to find a bed. He had a sense that both Dee and Greene were staring hard at his retreating back, but he did not care.

Bylot staggered to the room he'd occupied before his voyage with Davis. Could he skry? Had he communicated with angels? He didn't know. It had all seemed very real while it was happening, but now? Was it just some trick of Greene's, pulling up half-forgotten memories of his mystical readings at Clerkenwell? What of the prophecies? Madami had said he would suffer loneliness. Well he had already—so many of those he knew and cared for were dead. She had also said he would become an explorer but not be recognized. It was not difficult to guess Bylot would go on other voyages. Recognition, or not, would have to await the results of them.

Uriel had said Bylot would be happy twice. Once he already had been—with Evelyn before the plague took her. Greene could have known or guessed that. And again when his dreams were answered by the earthly sphere? That made little sense. What were Bylot's dreams? To know the world, and how else could that be achieved other than on the earthly sphere itself? It was all so confusing.

Bylot lay back on the cushions. Tomorrow he would leave Mortlake. He had intended only to give Dee the fire rock and had been drawn into the skrying by his curiosity. But there was nothing else for him here. He had learned the arts of navigation and practised them with Davis. Now he would go and seek his own way.

# 9

## Preparations

The morning after the skrying, Bylot left Mortlake for the city. Dee made no attempt to stop him, merely thanking him for the fire rock and wishing him well. Bylot was glad to be away, but he was disappointed too. He had half-expected Dee to ask him to undertake a voyage to discover the fourth element. By the time he was back in the bustle of London's streets, however, he had convinced himself that he was better off seeking his fortune on his own.

Bylot rented a modest room in an inn close to St. Paul's church and spent his first few days luxuriating in a bed that did not sway to the motion of a ship, sampling all manner of fresh food, and attending to matters with the notary who had kept his affairs in order during the long voyage.

Eventually, Bylot's mind turned to the future. A few inquiries among the seafaring community brought him one sunny morning to the door of a modest house in the east of London, close to the walls of the Tower. His knock was answered by a tall, middle-aged woman, wearing a long, red dress that showed signs of age. Her hair was tied back, accentuating her high cheekbones, and she gave Bylot a look that suggested she would put up with no nonsense.

"Good morning," Bylot said with a slight bow. "I was told that Master Henry Hudson resides here, and was wondering if it might be possible to speak with him."

"He's not in," the woman said bluntly.

"Then perhaps I might call back at a more convenient time?"

"You won't have to," the woman said, looking over Bylot's left shoulder. Bylot followed her gaze and saw a man approaching. He was walking briskly and was deep in conversation with a boy of about twelve. Bylot smiled. The man was older than when Bylot had last seen him and he was not certain he would have recognized the long face or pointed beard. But there was no mistaking the green coat with the dark fur collar. It was undoubtedly the one he had seen on the man who stood beside John Davis in Founders Hall seven years before.

Henry Hudson climbed the steps to his front door and looked inquiringly at his visitor.

"Robert Bylot." Bylot repeated his bow. "At your service."

"Do not, young man, go offering your service to all and sundry without knowing what it entails. But I am pleased to meet you. My name, as I am sure you know, is Henry Hudson. This is my son John ..."

"My preference is to be called Jack," the boy interrupted.

"A common name, and you exhibit the manners to go with it." John Hudson looked abashed. His father grinned at Bylot and continued. "The good lady who opened the door to you is my beloved wife, Katherine."

John Hudson bowed, and Bylot was surprised to see the woman blush.

"Now," Henry Hudson went on, "what would your business with me be?"

"I was told of you by John Davis, with whom I have lately voyaged to the Moluccas."

"Poor Davis. You were there when he died?"

"Yes."

"Then you must come in and tell me all the sad details. He was a good friend."

Hudson ushered everyone into the hall, where he removed his coat.

"John, I believe you should be undertaking some studying. Katherine, would you bring Master Bylot and myself some warmed wine. I fear I shall need some fortification when I hear his story."

Hudson led Bylot into a tidy, well-decorated parlour. The pair sat on matching, high-backed chairs on either side of a simple stone hearth with an unlit fire. After the wine was brought and poured, Bylot told Hudson the story of John Davis's last voyage. When he had finished, there was the glint of a tear in the other man's eye.

"He was a wonderful navigator and a great man. He should not have come to such an end. He taught me all I know of navigation and exploration."

"He taught me much as well," Bylot said. "And he spoke highly of you."

"Thank you for that and for bringing me this tale. Is there anything I can do for you in return?"

"I want to sail through the Furious Overfall," Bylot said, impulsively.

"Ah. So you listened to Davis's story."

"More than just a story. You saw it, too."

"I did."

"And do you think the Overfall leads into the Straits of Anian?" Bylot asked.

"I am certain of it," Hudson replied. "The Overfall is much the same latitude as some say Drake's entrance to the west."

"You have read Drake's secret journal?"

"No, I have only heard tell of it."

"I have read it in part."

Hudson stared at Bylot in amazement. "How?"

"Dee showed it to me when I stayed with him. It places the eastern entrance to the Straits of Anian near 58 degrees and the distance around some 1,500 miles."

"Fifteen hundred miles! That is but two weeks sail with a fair wind. Had Davis known that, we might yet have attempted the Overfall for all its terrors. Still, I am certain I saw the waters of the Pacific where they flood into our own Atlantic."

"Then you plan to return?"

Hudson looked thoughtful for a moment. "I do, but my plans are as yet not widely known. I would ask you to keep them to yourself."

"Of course," Bylot said eagerly.

"I have been in discussion with Sir Thomas Smythe and the others in his Company. They are prepared to finance voyages of exploration."

"That is wonderful." Bylot could barely contain his rising excitement.

"Indeed it is, but it is not simple. Some in the company, Digges and Wolstenholme particularly, wish to attempt other routes."

"All other routes have been disproven."

"I agree with you." Hudson took a long drink of wine. "But the men with the money make the plans. I have agreed next year to attempt the route over the North Pole."

"May I sail with you, nonetheless?"

"I'm afraid not, my friend," Hudson explained. "It is Smythe's voyage and he picks the crew. I had the devil's own job persuading him to allow me to take John as ship's boy. But do not fear, this is but a diversion."

"Then why attempt it?"

"I sail to prove to men of little imagination that it cannot be done. I suspect that Smythe and the others, once the Pole proves impossible, will push for an attempt at the Northeastern Passage around Muscovy."

"That too will fail."

"I know, and I shall not push so hard that I become trapped in the ice. With a little luck I shall find some whalefish to satisfy Smythe's financial greed, and then I shall be free to attempt the Overfall, perhaps in the summer of '09. By then I shall be able to pick my own crew and I would be glad if you would join me—if you might still be interested."

"I would be honoured, indeed."

"Good. In the meantime, I can put you in touch with some men who can fill your time with short voyages to Amsterdam, Brest and so forth, so that you may hone your skills and not die of boredom while I am gone."

Bylot and Hudson spent the rest of the morning talking of the sea, their lives and their hopes. By the time Katherine called them for lunch, they were firm friends.

So Bylot voyaged in coastal waters while Hudson sailed

north in 1607. He did the same in the following year as Hudson attempted a passage to the northeast. On both occasions, Hudson returned with stories and reports of commercial fisheries, but no passage to Cathay.

While Henry and John were away, Bylot spent much time with Katherine, whom he came to know as a strong, self-willed woman. He wondered with a touch of sadness if, had Evelyn lived, she might have developed into such a person. He also met Hudson's two other sons, Richard, who was already a man and talked of adventures and making his fortune in the Indies, and Oliver, who was still only an infant. For the first time in his life, Bylot felt he was a part of a real family.

In the winter of 1609, Bylot accepted a short voyage to the African coast, certain that he would be returned in time for Hudson's third voyage. Unfortunately, shipwreck and a three-month struggle for survival on the harsh desert coast before the crew were rescued meant that he did not reach England until high summer. He discovered that Hudson had gone to Holland from where he had led an expedition to the west. Bylot was confused at Hudson's change in plans, and distraught at the missed opportunity. However, he was delighted when Hudson returned in the fall with no success to report. Hudson, on the other hand, was very low.

"I could not wait for you, Robert, all thought you dead. In any case, Smythe was delaying and the Hollanders offered me a new ship and crew."

"But you did not attempt the Overfall."

Hudson sighed. "I did not. It turns out Smythe's hand was in the mix after all. He had schemed with the mate on the voyage—one Robert Juet, with whom I have had difficulties before—and it was all a device to take the costs of the voyage out of the Hollander's pockets instead of his own. But the Hollanders make a poor crew. They would not sail to the frozen lands, and so we were forced to explore to the south, following some mad idea that there is a way through the continent below the fiftieth parallel. We discovered much, but not the big prize. Sometimes I despair of ever seeing the Overfall again."

"Next year," Bylot said hopefully. "Surely then Smythe will attempt the Overfall."

"I don't know," Hudson rubbed his eyes wearily, "and in truth I do not know if I have it in me any more."

Bylot was shocked to hear his friend speak so negatively. "What of your dreams?"

"Dreams? I am getting too old for dreams, Robert. I have voyaged continuously for three years now. John I have had with me, but Richard has become a man in that time and I have not seen it. Little Oliver does not recognize me as his father each time I return. Katherine still encourages and says I must go, but I can see in her eyes that she would prefer I stay. And I am become of that mind. My bones ache in the cold and I cannot abide the strain of commanding such villains as I have any more. I think I must step aside and let a younger man go. Perhaps yourself."

"You are tired. A few weeks rest and good food and you will be yourself again. The dreams will return and we shall sail next summer."

"Perhaps," Hudson said without conviction.

Bylot fretted through the winter, unable to lift Hudson

from his black moods for more than a few days at a time. One raw February morning in 1610, a messenger delivered a note to Bylot's meagre lodgings. A handwriting he did not recognize requested his presence at an address in the commercial part of town. Bylot did not know the address, but he had no doubt the note had originated with Dee. He had lived the previous three years half-expecting a summons that would offer him an adventure in search of the fourth and final element. On his way across town, Bylot struggled to decide what his response to Dee's offer should be. Hudson had not committed to a voyage the following summer, but Bylot still had hopes he would. How could he agree to go without his friend? He was still wavering between acceptance and rejection when he stood before the pillared grand entrance to the three-storey house specified in the note. He was therefore shocked to be ushered into the presence of Thomas Smythe.

"Ah, young Bylot. We meet for a third time." Smythe stepped forward and grasped Bylot's hand. "I have been remiss in not sooner offering a home to your burgeoning talents—you are becoming quite well known as a navigator of promise. I can plead only the pressures of a life of commerce. However, a mutual friend has recently returned you to my notice and I have a proposition that I hope will interest you. Have a seat. May I offer you some wine?"

Stunned by the barrage of compliments and hospitality, Bylot obediently sat and accepted some hot wine. "A mutual friend?" he managed at length.

"Seems you are not without some influence—but to business. You have heard of Master Hudson's recent ventures?"

"I have."

"Good. So you know then that he has discovered the Straits of Anian."

"What?"

Smythe laughed. "I must apologize. I set out deliberately to shock you, but it is true. Oh, Hudson has not sailed *through* the passage, but he has tried to the north, south and east. By elimination, all that is left is the west and that is through Davis's Furious Overfall. Hudson is convinced of it. Even Davis said that, with the right ship and crew, the passage would be easy. The tides that have been seen flowing from the Overfall must come from a body of water so large that it can be none other than the Pacific Ocean. Merely be of stout heart and sail against those tides, and success is assured."

Bylot knew all this and more, from his friendship with both Davis and Hudson, but why was Smythe telling him? He decided to play Smythe's game and see where it led. "Why then, if it is so easy, has it not been done?"

"Many reasons—Davis was prevented from returning by the Armada, Frobisher was too concerned with his search for gold, Weymouth lacked the mettle. Now is the time and Hudson is the man."

"What if he does not wish to be the man?"

Smythe's smile returned. "Do not worry on that note, Master Hudson will be persuaded. But as to your role. Henry Hudson is a great man and well up to this adventure. We will provide him a good ship and he already has the makings of an experienced crew from his previous voyages. But he is a difficult combination of wilfulness and weakness. He has strong ideas about which course to take, but can be too easily swayed from it by others, a characteristic that has brought him grief before. Hudson needs be more of a Drake, so I need men aboard to stiffen his resolve should it waver.

"I will place one such, Master Peter Coleburne, as adviser. But he is not a navigator and his position as my man will be well known, thus I fear that his opinion will be too easily discounted in a crisis. What I require is someone aboard who knows the sea and whose relationship to me is—shall we say—unexplained."

"And you wish me to fill that role?"

"Exactly."

Bylot's mind raced with the possibilities. If Smythe were right and Hudson did lead an expedition to the Overfall, Bylot did not need Smythe's offer—his friend had already guaranteed him a place on the voyage. But Bylot was unconvinced by Smythe's conviction that Hudson would sail. The explorer was tired and leaning strongly toward a quiet life with his family. If that happened, then Bylot's only chance at the Overfall was to accept the offer being put to him.

Bylot didn't trust Smythe—the man always seemed to have agendas that he kept to himself. What would he be committing himself too in agreeing to be Smythe's man on the voyage? Was what he was being offered—a chance to be part of discovering one of the last great unknowns on the surface of the planet—worth the leap of faith that he could control events sufficiently to support Henry Hudson and personally benefit from the voyage?

"Yes," Bylot said at last. "I will go."

# The Alchemist's Dream

Ψ

Bylot retreated for several days after his meeting with Smythe. He could not face Hudson and needed time to think through his actions. He was no clearer in his mind when Hudson showed up at his door.

Bylot ushered him in and Hudson began without pre-amble. "I sail this summer for the Overfall. Will you come with me?"

"Of course! But what has changed your mind?"

"Much. Smythe has been most generous."

"Generous?" It was not a term Bylot associated with Smythe.

"Yes. I am much in debt from my previous voyages. They were sponsored by Smythe, but he always managed to create accounting that left me poorer than when I began. I thought to escape that in sailing for the Hollanders, but Smythe's hand was in that, too. Men of commerce do not attend closely to nations' borders. So Smythe has offered me one last chance to clear my debts. He is even prepared to board Katherine and the boys in one of his apartments while I am gone."

"That, at least, is generous."

"Robert," Hudson said with an ironic smile, "how I wish I had the simple views of youth. Smythe's apartment is in the Tower of London. It is generous on the surface, but beneath lies the imprisonment of my family against my successful return."

"That is unconscionable!"

Hudson's smile broke into a laugh—the first Bylot had

heard from him in many weeks. "It is indeed, but we can expect no more from the likes of Smythe. In any case, that is not my primary reason for undertaking one final voyage. Last Wednesday eve, I had a visitor. Someone you know, I believe."

"Who?"

"One Henry Greene."

Bylot gasped. "I know him. He is Dee's creature."

"Indeed he is, and Dee has no love for Smythe. I must admit that I am not strong in the ways of the Magus, preferring the solidity of a deck beneath my feet to the wings of angels. However, Greene showed me something utterly remarkable—a map of the world."

Bylot's memory swept back to Dee's talk of maps, and the mysterious one that supposedly showed the unknown parts of the world in impossible detail. "The portolan!" he blurted it out before he could stop himself.

"I see you are familiar with it. You heard of it from Dee?"

Bylot nodded, not trusting himself to speak.

"And have you seen it?"

Bylot shook his head.

"It is truly remarkable, even in the rough copy I was shown. It was crude and hurriedly drawn, without constant scale and missing many elements, but it was a map of the world such as no one could imagine today! I could discern the Mediterranean, the outline of Africa and the peninsulas of Asia. It showed a passable outline of the easternmost coast of the Americas. Inevitably, as soon as I was certain of what I was seeing, my eye was drawn to the earth's extremities.

"To the south lay the huge *Terra Australis,* which no one from Europe has yet visited, but that was drawn in such detail that I am certain it must have been based on some lost voyages of which we know not."

Bylot felt more excited than he had since his magical conversations with Evelyn as a child. After all he had been through, here it was at last—a chance to go on a real voyage of exploration. And not only that—to discover and use the mysteries of the fabled world portolan! Bylot's attention was riveted on his friend as he continued.

"What made the breath catch in my throat was the northern portion of the sketch. It had obviously been of importance to the artist as it was drawn to a larger scale, encompassing almost half the page, and was presented in greater detail than the rest. The Scandinavian lands were there, as was Greenland. Much open sea was shown to the north and around Russia but, as I know from experience, these waters are ice clogged. To the west lay the strait I sailed with Davis and the northern parts of the Americas. Clearly marked were not one, but two passages to the Pacific."

"Two!"

"Indeed. The copyist had, in his enthusiasm to emphasis the northern lands, come near to running out of paper in this northwest corner. To compensate, he had again reduced the scale. Even so, he had failed to find enough paper to take his map as far as the west coast of the Americas. Nevertheless, there was no mistaking what he was showing. Since the map lacked either latitude or longitude lines, exact positions were difficult to determine, but, from a comparison of known features, I could draw some deductions.

"The entrance to the northernmost passage lay close to the northern shore of Greenland, as much as I could judge, far to the north of even the point reached by Davis and myself. It was narrow and wound amongst many irregular islands. There was not room to show its egress into the Pacific Ocean, but an arrow, inscribed at the page's margin, unmistakably indicated its continuation."

"Is it navigable?" Bylot asked.

"I think not. In latitude, it must be close to that of the northern Muscovy coast and that, I know, is closed by ice. The southerly route, however, is an old friend. It lay approximately opposite the southernmost tip of Greenland, at a location I took immediately to represent the Furious Overfall. It was shown as a straight passage emptying out into a vast sea with no eastern shore."

"You are convinced the map was genuine?"

"I am convinced it was based on a reality. It was too outrageous not to be. Greene spun me some tale of long-dead Arab mystics and Trojans rescuing ancient knowledge, but that is of consequence only to Dee's fantasies. The map shows the Straits of Anian, Robert! And we can sail through them."

The pair sat in silence, overwhelmed by the possibilities. Hudson's eyes gleamed with excitement. Bylot felt so alive, he was aware of every beat of his heart. Smythe and his games were forgotten. Bylot didn't need them any more.

"Do you really think we can sail through?" Bylot asked, not fully trusting himself to believe the possibilities.

"I am certain."

"Do you have the map?"

"I have it here." Hudson tapped his forehead. "The paper

copy, Greene kept. Will you come with me?"

"I will." For the second time in as many weeks, Bylot agreed to undertake the voyage.

Ψ

The following weeks were a blur of frantic activity. While Hudson collected charts and signed on the crew, Bylot rushed across the city ordering food and equipment and ensuring that their vessel, the *Discovery*, was seaworthy. They were only days away from sailing when Bylot returned to his lodgings one evening to find John Dee sitting in his parlour.

"How did you get in?"

"Paths through the physical world are easy," said the Magus. "It is in the spiritual realm where the challenge lies. I hear you are to undertake a new voyage."

"I suspect you have come for more than well wishing."

Dee's wrinkled face broke into a smile. "You are to go as Smythe's man, I hear."

"You hear many things."

"I keep an eye out, in a friendly way."

"It was you who engineered my position on the ship."

Dee nodded.

"But you detest Smythe and all he stands for! He would not listen to you."

"A cat may be skinned in many ways. I have a favour to ask of you."

Bylot sighed. "You wish me to find the fourth element?"

"I do." Dee reached beneath the folds of his cloak, produced a rolled page and offered it to Bylot. "Here is a copy of the location from Trithemius's *Steganographia*. I think you will be close and it should be sufficient in detail."

Bylot took the document and unrolled it. It showed a sketch of a wide river flowing into a sea in front of three rounded hills. Around the edge were numbers and writing in Dee's mystical language.

"Do not concern yourself with the writing," Dee said. "The figures give the location, but, I suspect, with greater accuracy than your poor instruments will allow. The picture must be the thing to guide once you know yourself to be close."

Bylot suddenly felt overwhelmed by the growing complexity of the voyage—Smythe, Hudson and now Dee all had claims on his loyalty. He wished for the voyage to begin so that he could immerse himself in the hard work of sailing and navigating. "Must I serve three masters?"

"It is not difficult if there is no conflict between their desires."

"I shall attempt what you wish to the best of my ability and only if the achievement does not harm any for whom I care."

"I can ask no more." Dee stood. It was obvious from his slowness and awkward movements that his joints pained him considerably. "The body is cursed with decay. I sometimes yearn for the spirit to be freed. But I shall await my time.

"I have something else for you." Dee reached again into his cloak and produced a flask. "For the element." He delved again and brought out the alchemist's globe that Bylot had seen before in Dee's study. "Its look belies its sturdiness, but do not treat it as you did that day by my hearth. Should the materials within and around the earthly sphere mix, a great power is unleashed. Keep it well and look into its depths should you need guidance."

Bylot accepted the globe and stared at its intricate carvings, swirling liquids and four sealed elements at the centre. What did it all mean? Why was he being given such a precious gift and what was there in the depths that could possibly guide him?

"I must go now," Dee said. "My weak body requires its rest. Henry."

Henry Greene emerged as if by magic from the dark corner shadows where he had observed and listened.

"Good day, Master Bylot," he greeted the surprised man. "Do not worry yourself. I shall see the Magus safe home. I wish you luck in your venture."

Before Bylot could formulate an answer, the pair were out the door into the darkness. Bylot sat and looked deep into the mysterious globe. Perhaps it *would* one day guide him, but for now, he wished it could answer his many questions.

# 10

## Master's Mate

The voyage began auspiciously. The *Discovery* was seen off shortly after dawn on April 17 from St. Katherine's Pool beneath the Tower by none other than Prince Henry who stood waving regally, surrounded by the expedition's backers—Smythe, Digges and Wolstenholme. Only Hudson was not caught up in the enthusiasm. He stood aloof on the quarter deck, accompanied by his son, John, gazing hard at the Tower, hoping for a last glimpse of Katherine and Oliver.

Over the past weeks, Bylot, who sailed as leading seaman, had come to know a little of some of his twenty-two fellow voyagers. Even before the lines were cast, there were factions—pro- and anti-Hudson—forming on the ship. Many of those who favoured Hudson had sailed with him before. They included John, who was now a well-built youth of nearly fifteen and fiercely loyal to his father. The ship's carpenter, Phillip Staffe, had accompanied Hudson on two previous voyages and was also unquestionably loyal to the captain. He was a large man, well capable of hauling heavy timbers into place, and his bluff, straightforward view of the world and man's doings in it were refreshing, although Bylot suspected that he annoyed some crew members. The quartermaster, John King; the surgeon, Edward Wilson;

the mathematician, Thomas Wydehouse; and the cooper, Sylvanus Bond, were also solidly Hudson men and were frequently invited to dine with the captain.

On the other side, the ship's mate, Robert Juet, although he had sailed twice before with Hudson, maintained a distance. He was not hostile yet—in fact, he spoke strongly in favour of Hudson's goals in discussions—but he could not be called a friend of any in Hudson's clique. Bylot strongly suspected Juet was Smythe's man. Juet was tight with able seamen William Wilson and John Thomas, and with Abacuk Prickett, who travelled as a passenger. Prickett, Bylot also began to suspect, might have ties to Smythe.

The obvious Smythe man, however, was Peter Coleburne, who knew nothing of ships and the sea, and hovered uselessly around in his ruff and hose, getting in the way and asking stupid questions. The remainder of the crew seemed an average cross-section of nautical men, content to do their jobs as long as the captain required it and they were fed and kept relatively safe.

As the *Discovery* slipped from the shore, Bylot wondered as much about the tensions that they carried with them as the unknown lands into which they were to venture. The demands of Smythe and Dee weighed on his mind. He vowed that, whatever happened, they would never compromise his friendship with Hudson.

Four days after their send-off, the *Discovery* was docked at Gravesend, down the Thames River from London, awaiting the tide. The morning watch was but an hour old and there was still an hour before dawn and the tide that would take them out into the wide estuary. Bylot had been unable to sleep since the watch bell, and stood at the rail, staring at the moonlit, black water lapping the hull below him. A scuffle of feet made him turn in time to see a shadowy figure with a sea bag climbing the gangway. Stepping forward to challenge the stranger, Bylot became aware of another figure by his side.

"Do not be concerned, Robert," Henry Hudson said. "We have a passenger joining us."

"Who?"

"A friend," the stranger said in a soft voice that sent a chill down Bylot's spine.

"What is he doing here? Why bring him along?"

"Hush, Robert. Let us go to the great cabin where we can discuss this in peace."

Bylot followed the two shapes aft. Only two men slept at deck level aft of the mainmast, Phillip Staffe in the tool room fore of the mizzen mast and Hudson in the great cabin behind it.

Once settled, Henry Greene removed his cloak and smiled at Bylot.

"Why is he here?" Bylot asked.

"He has knowledge we might need," Hudson said. "He has seen the portolan."

"Then why must you secret him aboard in the dead of night?"

"There we have a squabble not of my doing," Hudson replied. "Sir Thomas Smythe would not have approved of Henry Greene for his association with Doctor Dee, although it matters naught in our venture."

"Coleburne will not take kindly to this."

"Do not concern yourself over him. It is in hand. But will you join us for a goblet of wine?"

"I think not." Bylot excused himself and returned to the open deck, feeling immensely uncomfortable. Things were becoming oddly complex. He had assumed that as soon as the *Discovery* sailed, things would be simple and he would escape Dee and Smythe's influence. With Greene and Coleburne aboard, however, it would not be that easy.

Bylot need not have worried about the latter. The following day, the *Discovery* hove to off the Isle of Sheppey and hailed a pinke passing upriver to London. Under Hudson's orders, Peter Coleburne was bundled onto the merchantman along with a letter that, Bylot later discovered, gave but a weak excuse for his departure. In reality, although Hudson was certain other of Smythe's men were placed among his crew, the captain was minimizing their influence and sending a message that, powerless as he was with Katherine and Oliver in the Tower, he would not submit his on-board authority to such a useless passenger as Coleburne. The note made no mention of Greene's arrival, although it was certain that Coleburne would make Smythe aware of it.

Little occurred for the next few weeks to disturb the routine and Bylot was lulled into thinking that all might be well. The weather held fair and the winds sped them north along the coast. Bylot had little chance for protracted discussions with the busy Hudson, but enjoyed some time with his son. John was already a competent navigator and his enthusiasm to learn reminded Bylot of himself in earlier years.

The only worry Bylot had was a change in Juet's attitude. Since Greene's arrival, Juet's negativity had blossomed. He spent much of his time in petty complaints that could cause only trouble. Bylot could see no sense to it and eventually decided it was merely the man's nature.

When they were held up by fog at Iceland, the crew bathed in the hot springs at Louise Bay and caught many fowl and fish. The only negative was the eruption of Mount Hekla, which, the older seamen said, presaged foul weather.

On the morning of May 24, Bylot was standing on the deck, watching the black coast of Iceland come and go as the fog banks rolled past.

"It's consumption."

Bylot turned to see the surgeon, Edward Wilson, approaching. "What?"

"The gunner, John Williams—he has the consumption." Wilson wiped his hands on his jerkin and leaned on the rail.

"Are you sure?"

"There can be no doubt. He coughs bright blood and that is a death warrant, for sure. He'll be lucky to see Christ's Mass. We must return him to England."

"No!" Both men turned to see Greene standing behind them. "We must continue."

"You are not to say," Wilson sneered. Much of the crew had not taken to Greene. As a passenger, he had no duties to perform and his arrogant nature rubbed many the wrong way. Several, Edward Wilson among them, made no attempt to disguise their feelings.

"That man should not have come. He must have known he was sick afore we sailed. It was his choice—let him bear the consequences. We are engaged in matters too important to let a single fool prevent us. He is but a gunner. We will have little need of his services."

"Fool or not, he is a man and what man does not deserve the right to die at home if it be possible? And do not you talk of unnecessary numbers. What do you account for, but a few pounds of useless meat?"

Greene stepped forward. "We can do as well without a butcher, too."

Wilson pushed Greene hard in the chest and Bylot was surprised at how strongly Greene held his ground. The two men's faces were inches apart.

"Do not make an enemy of me," Greene snarled.

"Do not presume that I fear you and your mystical nonsense," Wilson replied. "A butcher you may call me, but I follow the new natural philosophies that will one day banish your pitiful magic from our lives and illuminate the dark corners where your like dwells. Be gone with your angels and—"

Greene's fist flashed up from his side and Wilson staggered back against the rail. Without hesitation, he rebounded, catching Greene a blow on the temple. In an instant the two men were locked in combat. Juet and some others quickly gathered to watch. Bylot tried to intervene with little effect.

"What goes on here?" Hudson appeared from the stern. "Juet, Bylot, separate those men."

Eventually, Greene and Wilson stood defiant before the captain.

"What is the meaning of this?"

"This creature you saw fit to bring aboard," Wilson began angrily, "is less than human. We have a man close to death below and he argues for continuing with our voyage."

Greene spat a bloody tooth onto the deck, but spoke calmly. "The man will die shortly whether he lies in our hold or a feather bed in Nonesuch Palace. If we return to England we lose this year and, perhaps, our chance."

"Greene has a point." Hudson addressed Wilson. "Would you give up all for a dying man?"

"I would. Any man here," Wilson swept an arm to encompass the gathered crew, "even dying, is worth more than a mere line on a map and certainly more than this skryer." He spat the final word and a grumble of agreement rolled around the assembled men.

"I will have none of this," Hudson said. "Men die to achieve great things. Juet, as soon as the fog clears, set a course westward."

"Aye," Juet said as Greene smirked in victory. Then more quietly, he added. "Beware that magician, mates. I fear Hudson brought him on to crack my credit with you."

Hudson, who had begun to walk away, spun back and faced his mate. "You shall speak against your captain, Juet? I will not turn back for a dead man, but I will to put you ashore to shift for yourself until some fishing smack should see fit to take you back."

Several of the crew gasped at the anger in Hudson's voice.

"Robert, attend to me in my cabin."

Bylot followed Hudson as he pushed his way through the men.

Once in the great cabin, Hudson was a different man.

"They are like children," he explained, all anger gone, "and are easily swayed. Juet knows that and I must not allow him to gain too much control over them. I have had trouble with his manipulations before and I will not allow them to destroy this voyage."

"But they do not like Greene and you took his side most smartly," Bylot rejoined.

Hudson laughed. "I did, but there is a world of difference between Greene and Juet. Greene, for all his mystery, is of like mind to me as to our purpose. He was right about the sick man, Robert—we cannot abandon this great enterprise on one man's account. It is my only chance. Juet merely swings with the wind. He saw the crew swing to the surgeon and went with it. As for Edward Wilson, he is a good enough surgeon but he has a tongue that would wrong his best friend. He knows not when to hold his peace."

Bylot kept silent. He had no wish to take sides over an issue that was already resolved.

Eventually Hudson continued. "I am glad you came along. Apart from John, you are the only person I can talk to. I can rely upon your judgment as being unbiased. I hope you will not mind if I use you in such a way."

"Not at all," Bylot said, swallowing his guilt. "I am flattered by your confidence."

"Excellent. Now, we had best prepare. I felt a breeze and perhaps it presages a break in this damnable fog. We must be prepared to take advantage."

Bylot returned to his duties on deck. It was near noon and, if the fog cleared, it would soon be time for the day's navigational readings.

# The Alchemist's Dream

Ψ

The voyage progressed smoothly, but Bylot heard grumblings in the darkness below decks. The Atlantic crossing was no better or worse than many another and by the first week of July they were past Resolution Island and well into the Furious Overfall.

The ship was held fast by ice when the crew's tempers finally boiled over. Bylot had just taken the day's position to Hudson and the pair were talking outside the great cabin with several crewmen nearby.

"Well, Robert," Hudson gloated. "We are 300 miles farther into the Overfall than any Englishman has yet ventured!"

"Much good it will do us if we are all to die in the ice." Abacuk Prickett whispered, but his voice carried clearly to the pair.

"Do not worry, Master Prickett," Hudson said calmly. "The ice will release us soon enough."

But Prickett would not be silenced. "Had I one hundred pounds in gold to my name, I would happily give ninety to be home at this moment."

Before Hudson could reply, Phillip Staffe commented, "Some throw money away too easily. I would not give ten for the same result."

A general hubbub then erupted, with many of the men around taking either Prickett's side or Staffe's. Eventually Hudson stepped in and called for an assembly of the crew by the mainmast.

"I understand," Hudson said when all were present,

"that there is some desire among you to return home." A few men mumbled agreement. "Well," Hudson went on, "let us put it to a vote. Those in favour of returning home, raise your hands."

Prickett and a couple of others held up their hands.

"And those in favour of continuing."

Every other hand rose.

"Then it is resolved. We shall continue west as soon as the ice releases us."

Afterward, Hudson proudly boasted to Bylot of the way he had averted trouble, but Bylot was not happy. What Prickett had said was close to mutiny and that was the worst offense possible on board a ship. The captain of any ship was near to God within his domain. To maintain his mastery, a captain was expected to make clear decisions on all matters, even if those decisions were misguided. Bylot worried that giving the crew the final say in such an important choice as abandoning the voyage or not might seriously undermine Hudson's authority.

This was the first time that Bylot had seen Hudson in command, and he was a different person than the friend Bylot had come to know in London. Bylot began to understand Smythe's view that there was not enough Drake in Hudson. Drake had ruled his ship with an iron hand, not shying away from executing men who stood against him. It had been hard, but had he not done so, he could never have brought them through the adventures he had. Bylot did not see that sort of iron in Hudson's soul. Perhaps he was too generous a man to be harsh and, while generosity of spirit was mostly a fine characteristic, Bylot secretly hoped they would not find themselves in a situation where it might be the death of them all.

At length the ice released them, and the Discovery continued into the unknown, although some of the crew continued to grumble. For another four weeks, they battled through the Overfall, naming features—an island they called Desire Provoketh, the Bay of God's Mercie, and, at Bylot's request and to his great joy, a promontory called Evelyn's Point. They avoided crashing into mountains of ice and fought free of entrapment when they could.

On August 3, they passed between two headlands that they named for the voyage's backers, Digges and Wolstenholme, and saw a great body of water ahead. They rested, finally, stocked up with fresh water and hunted what game they could. They found many cairns that the savages of the area had filled with birds, but Hudson was in such a rush to continue that there was no chance to collect them.

Throughout August, they followed a coastline that trended broadly south. There was much discussion as to whether this would eventually lead to California and the Spanish, but Bylot held his opinion in reserve. Their exit from the Overfall did not match what he knew of Drake's description of the western entrance to the Straits of Anian. Also, by his calculations, they had a considerable distance to go west before they reached the longitude of California. However, their course did take them closer to the location of Dee's fourth element.

In September, they came into a shallow bay. Hudson turned back north and then west several times, but each turn led to a northward trending shoreline. Juet openly jeered at Hudson's boast that they would be in Bantam by Candlemass.

On September 10, Bylot dined in the great cabin. After the meal, the conversation turned to their situation and the possibility of having to overwinter nearby.

"I still think we can escape west before the ice closes us in," Hudson said. "But if not, then we will find a sheltered bay and wait out the cold." Through the meal, Hudson had been happier than Bylot had seen him for some time and it worried him. It seemed almost a fevered happiness and Bylot was concerned at the easy way his friend dismissed the possibility of what would certainly be a very hard winter.

"Do you think we can manage a winter?" Bylot asked. "We are not overly well provisioned, and we do not know the country hereabouts. Juet, Prickett and some others are certain to prove difficult."

"Difficult!" Bylot was shocked by the violence of Hudson's response. His happiness evaporated in a moment and anger overwhelmed him. "This flouting of my authority cannot go on." Hudson rose abruptly, knocking a goblet off the table. "I shall finish this here and now," he said, striding out of the cabin. Bylot followed, confused and worried at Hudson's sudden, unaccountable mood swing.

The crew was called on deck and Hudson addressed them. Bylot stood to one side, nervous at what the meeting might develop into.

"This is a mutinous crew," Hudson began. Some men looked at each other in confusion and Bylot's heart fell. "I have called you here this evening to determine the actions to be taken against the leader of the mutiny, Robert Juet, for the many slanders he has expressed against this voyage and my person."

"I welcome it," Juet interrupted arrogantly. "I have done naught to wrong any and there is much within these wooden walls that needs airing."

"Very well, then. To begin, when we were held by the Iceland fog, you spoke against my decision to continue—"

"On that occasion—"

"You will have a chance to reply," Hudson cut off Juet. "When we were icebound in the Overfall, you spoke against our continuance when, as ship's mate, you should have, with strength, taken your captain's part. These are serious enough charges and there are more, but I would ask if any others among you have cause to think the less of Juet."

Bennett Mathew, a man of great girth who was ship's cook and, because of the carrying voice that emanated from his huge frame, the man charged with relaying Hudson's orders to the crew, stepped forward. "I be but a poor cook and trumpet," he began in his west-country accent, "but I hears too and there be things said below deck that should not be said 'gin the captain of any ship and that I does not take to."

Several crew members were shuffling uncomfortably as Mathew went on. "As we come 'pon Iceland, I hears the mate talk with the boatswain, Francis Clements, saying as how there was to be the need for action and murder and that it would prove bloody."

A gasp rose from the assembled crew. Juet stood stoically looking hard at Mathew.

"Is there more, Master Cook?" Hudson asked.

"Aye, sir. There be. Upon the fog releasing us, I hears the

mate say that at any time he could take the ship over and head us all back home."

Mathew stood back. Juet stared at him, but the big man met his gaze.

"At the same time as Master Mathew speaks," Arnal Ludlowe spoke up, "the mate said that we needs to keep muskets charged and swords ready for there would be use for them afore the voyage was over. Our carpenter was with me."

Phillip Staffe nodded agreement. "It is true what Arnal says and, what is more, at the time we were much pestered by the ice in the Overfall, Juet went about the crew talking of mutiny and discouragement, a view that had a poor effect on those who are timid at our venture."

"Thank you all," Hudson said. "There is obviously much with which I can take Master Juet to task. Not least is that he now speaks against our continuing, saying that we are trapped in a poor bay and will all die of want when the snows come upon us—words that, like the ones of which Staffe spoke, are like to put the timid among the crew to a great fright. What say you to these charges?"

"I thank you for a chance to reply." Juet stepped forward and spoke with heavy sarcasm. Bylot expected a long and manipulative address to the crew's emotions and, possibly, a showdown with Hudson. It came to nothing. "But I shall say naught. Some of what you heard are damnable lies, yet I do admit to speaking in disaffection. Let the captain dispose of my punishment as he sees fit."

"Very well, then," Hudson said. "For these various base slanders against my name and against the position of captain, and for spreading dissent, discouragement and fear amongst the crew, I relieve you, Robert Juet, of the position of master's mate for the remainder of this voyage. For being a cohort and for poor performance of his duties, I also depose Francis Clements from the position of boatswain and, in his place, set up William Wilson who, I trust, shall perform his duties with due diligence.

"As for master's mate, I hereby elevate Robert Bylot to the position."

Bylot's jaw dropped open in astonishment. From being a quiet, background figure, he was being thrust into the limelight, in less than envious circumstances. "I cannot," he stammered.

"You can and you shall." Hudson cut him off. "There has been enough discussion. Go about your tasks and we shall continue with the voyage."

Bylot went forward in confusion, not only at his own dramatic change in circumstances but also at Hudson's behaviour. He had shown some firmness in decision making, but had it healed the rifts among the crew or deepened them?

# II

## Maps

The winter began badly with the long-awaited death of the gunner. For the most part, John Williams had born his illness bravely, even expressing good humour. However, after the ship became beset in October his mood deteriorated and his illness entered its final phase. Williams's decline mirrored the crew's distress at the prospect of a winter in such a barren place. Late on the morning watch of November 15, Williams was convulsed by a final fit of bloody coughing and expired. The crew buried him on a small knoll on the nearby shore.

Bylot was relieved that Williams was at peace and that his coughing no longer disturbed his every hour, but the sight of the bare mound of stones on the shore was a continual reminder of the fate that might await them all.

When the burial party returned to the ship, the crew gathered around the mainmast for the traditional auctioning of the dead man's possessions. There was much interest in Williams's heavy grey cloak, and many coveted it as an item that would serve them well in the coming cold months. Bylot himself planned to bid upon it.

The auction proceeded rapidly in a cold wind blowing off the bay, with Prickett buying most of the clothing and Staffe a fish-gutting knife and powder horn. Anticipation was at a height when the cloak was finally held up.

Before anyone could announce a bid, Greene stepped forward and felt the weight of the material. "This will cut the wind and no doubt," he said to a general murmur of agreement. "It is of the quality of the Captain's fine green coat itself." Then Greene looked directly at Hudson. "I have a great desire for this cloak. I would take it as part payment for my attendance on this voyage."

Every eye fixed on Hudson. Bylot and the others knew that Greene, as a passenger not approved by Smythe, was due no wages and would thus be paid direct from Hudson's pocket.

Hudson waited an age during which time the wind seemed to get colder. Bylot toyed with his leather purse, heavy with the weight of the coin he had planned to bid.

Eventually, Hudson spoke. "Very well then, Henry. You shall have the cloak."

A gasp rose from the crew.

"No!" Phillip Staffe stepped forward. "Tradition demands that the gunner's possessions be auctioned to the crew and the money returned to his family."

"I shall recompense his family," Hudson said, ignoring Staffe's impertinence.

"That is not enough, Master Hudson. Each of us has as much need of a good cloak as Henry Greene—many more so since they work subject to the elements while he sits comfortable and warm in the great cabin. The cloak must be auctioned."

"Must! You presume to tell your captain what he *must* do? You get above yourself, master carpenter. I shall pay

Williams's family the worth of the cloak and Henry Greene shall have it. That is an end. Now, prepare your tools and materials and set about construction of a dwelling on shore for our winter habitation."

Hudson turned away, but Staffe stepped after him, his face red with fury. "It is not an end. I am not a house carpenter to be ordered about at your whim. For three weeks past, I have petitioned to begin our dwelling while the weather sat clement, and you have said no. Now, as the icy blast already sweeps in from the bay and snow-laden skies threaten, you order construction. We have, in previous adventures, lost an anchor and sat on rocks for full three watches on account of your not taking advice when it was due. Build your own house."

Hudson, who had half-turned back to listen to Staffe, spun fully around and landed a solid blow to the big man's cheek. Staffe staggered but regained his footing. His shoulders bunched and his fists clenched, and, for an awful moment, Bylot felt certain that Staffe would retaliate. If he did, Bylot had no idea what the consequences would be.

"Strike me," Hudson said in a voice laden with menace, "and you shall hang within a day."

For a moment, all possibilities hovered in a cold, impenetrable silence. Bylot, Juet, Greene—and the invisible Dee and Smythe—watched the two men as they eyed one another. This could be the end. If Staffe struck back, a line would be established and every man on deck would have to choose on which side he stood. The muskets and swords that Juet had told the crew to prepare would be put to bloody use.

A raucous laugh split the tension. Heads snapped around to look at Juet. "Here we are," he said through guffaws, "the only civilized men for a thousand miles in any direction, and all we can do is haggle and squabble over a dead man's coat. I hope we shall behave better when we reach the court of Cathay."

The tension cracked and bodies relaxed.

"Come, Henry," Juet continued, taking Greene by the elbow. "Did we not plan a trip to hunt for some fowl to supplement Master Mathew's admirable biscuits?"

"We did," Greene replied.

"Then there is no time like the present, before the snow falls and we are confined. Let us get our pieces and go."

The pair walked forward to the gunroom.

"I shall accompany you." Staffe said, following them.

"And most welcome you are, Master Staffe." Juet clapped the big man on the back and the trio ducked through the doorway. Bylot returned his gaze to Hudson who stood staring after them, a look of utter hate distorting his features.

For the rest of the day, Bylot's thoughts troubled him. What was happening aboard their small, isolated wooden world? Hudson, who abhorred violence, had struck and threatened to hang Staffe, one of the few among the crew who had been unquestioningly loyal. Staffe himself had challenged Hudson for the first time, and Juet, whom Bylot would have expected to try and profit from any discord or discomfort to Hudson, had defused the situation and possibly prevented a mutiny. Bylot expected inconsistency from a ship's crew, but Hudson's mood swings disturbed him deeply. If a captain could not be relied upon for consistency, all kinds of trouble were possible.

# The Alchemist's Dream

Ψ

The first light snow was falling the following day when Bylot was summoned to the great cabin. Staffe's anger had been assuaged and he had been persuaded to begin work on a shelter for the crew on shore. The noise of axes and hammers echoed from a nearby clearing in the trees.

Hudson sat, poring over the chart of the voyage. His mood was very different from the day previous. "Come in, Robert, come in. I have been meaning to seek your opinion for some time now. What think you of our circumstances?"

Bylot hesitated to voice the questions that had been swirling around his head the day before. With his apparently irrational mood swings, it was becoming very difficult to know how to react to Hudson.

"Come, come," Hudson said, smiling. "You are the only man I trust on this vessel. Speak freely."

Bylot swallowed hard and decided to confine his comments to practicalities. "In truth, I am much concerned. Smythe gave us only meagre provisions for our task and we have but six months' food remaining. Even with successful hunting, which is by no means certain, that will sustain us only until the spring. We know that the passage back out of the Overfall cannot be completed before mid-summer and there will be weeks after that to cross back over to England. I foresee dire want before we make home."

"That is your trouble, Robert! You do not think beyond the obvious. Why should we go home?"

"Why? What choice do we have? There is no way out of

this southern bay save the way we entered. Our voyagings in September and October proved that. Where else can we go?"

"That is what I mean. You do not think past the confines of this little bay. It is but a hiccup, an unfortunate sidetrack. Our error was in sailing south when we exited the Overfall. We should have sailed west. When the ice releases us, we need only sail north until open water once more presents itself to the west and we shall be in the Northern Ocean that, I am certain, connects with the strait that Drake discovered. By some calculations the distance can be only a few hundred miles, a matter of a few days' sail with a favourable wind. Look here at the map."

Bylot crossed to the table and peered at the chart. It showed the Overfall, the coast they had sailed south along, and Michaelmass Bay where they now sat.

Hudson pointed out features as he talked. "Here—the cape where the fowls breed that we called for Master Digges—that is nigh on 63 degrees. We now lie at close by 51 and have proven that this bay is closed near 55. As you well know, Drake found the westernmost entrance to the Straits of Anian at near 58 degrees. Therefore, we have 8 degrees of latitude that encompasses the one where Drake went. The passage must lie within. In the summer we shall find it, and the riches of Cathay shall be ours."

"But what if the larger water, too, is but a bay?"

"It is not."

"How can you be so sure?"

"Because I have another map," Hudson said, reaching over and pulling a sheet of paper from the chart drawer behind him. He laid it out on the table and Bylot leaned over to examine it.

The page was a torn fragment of a larger map. It was of recent vintage and clearly drawn, showing the southernmost tip of Greenland, Davis Strait and a large part of the American continent. At the extreme north, the land dissolved into a bewildering mass of islands and narrow passages. Farther south, Bylot recognized Frobisher's Strait, the Furious Overfall and the Great Sea they had entered with Michaelmass Bay pointing south from it. To the west, the larger body of water narrowed but continued as a passage at 58 degrees, where it was cut off by the edge of the paper.

"Where did you get this?" Bylot asked in awe.

Hudson smiled at his companion's surprise. "It is a copy of an ancient map of the world, a portolan—"

"The map that Greene spoke of?"

"Indeed."

"But you said the scale of that was mixed and the coast-lines unclear. This is of a single scale and shows exactly what we wish."

"It is remarkable, is it not? Greene claims he found other works in Dee's study that allowed him to clarify his first rough sketch."

"So that is why Greene accompanies us—and why you gave him Williams's cloak."

Hudson nodded. "The map did not come cheap and Greene has sold it piecemeal to the highest bidder. Unknown to me, other fragments went to Smythe. Some of them showed passages by the Pole and to the north of Muscovy, which explains Smythe's insistence on my earlier voyages there. I wish Greene had played fair from the beginning, but I suspect that is not the man's way. Even had he given me this final copy before we became stuck in this bay . . ." Hudson said wistfully. "But no matter, it shows the way out in the spring."

Bylot's mind was racing. Of course Greene had not produced the detailed map until now. If he had shown it earlier, Hudson would have sailed west from the Furious Overfall instead of south toward the location of Dee's fourth element. Bylot shook his head. Too many people were trying too hard to control this voyage. Smythe wanted riches, Dee wanted his water. Neither cared if it meant the hardships of a winter in Michaelmass Bay. Hudson was simply a pawn in the middle.

"You look troubled, Robert."

"I do not trust Greene."

"Nor I, but he serves our purpose."

Bylot wondered who was serving whose purpose, but he held silent.

"In any case," Hudson went on, "there is nothing we can do now. The elements hold us firm and we must do the best we can until the spring. Then we shall complete this task."

"Can you trust that Greene copied accurately?"

"You are too much the skeptic, Robert. To achieve greatness, must one not have a certain measure of faith? Greene seeks only profit."

Bylot seriously doubted that Greene's motives were ever as simple as that, but again he held his tongue.

"This is my final chance," Hudson said. "Will you stand by me, Robert?"

"I shall, but I must be free to admit doubts when they occur."

"Of course."

"Then the first is this. Even with this passage through Drake's Straits of Anian, we would starve before we reached the Pacific Ocean. If by some miracle we did get through, we should starve before we reached the closest succour with the Spanish in California, and there is no guarantee that they would help us. We can never cross to Cathay after a hard winter in these lands. Notwithstanding the map, I would argue now for a return home at the earliest the year will offer and an attempt another year to find the direct route through in one season in a properly provisioned vessel."

"That is not possible," Hudson said sadly. "Katherine and Oliver are being held captive against my success. If I return with this voyage incomplete, they shall never be released and I shall be forced to sail on for all time like some wandering Jew of the ocean, never permitted to rest."

"Surely not! You have done all one man can do and more. Smythe must allow you rest."

"Perhaps, but in my experience, Smythe and his like are not often overwhelmed by human kindness." Hudson pulled himself up and forced a smile to his lips. "There is no profit in kindness. If I succeed, I will release my family from Smythe's debt and be able to live my final years in peace and contentment. I will not see anyone wreck it.

"But enough moaning. I called you here this watch for other reasons. You are mate now and I would give you a gift in keeping with your station."

Hudson turned and lifted a bundle from the deck behind him. With a flourish, he handed Bylot Williams's grey cloak.

"But you gave this to Greene," Bylot stammered.

"Greene is not a man that his friends would trust with twenty shillings. And you saw yesterday how he went hunting in the company of Staffe while the heat of our anger was still in the air."

"But it was Juet who suggested the hunting as a way, I believe, to avoid bloodshed."

"Still and all, we face a hard winter and I cannot have my authority undermined. I was overhasty and this will teach him who is in command. I shall make my peace with Staffe. In truth," Hudson said thoughtfully, "few on this vessel are what they seem. There is more to Greene's presence than the map fragment.

"Before we set sail, I was much beaten down. Katherine and Oliver were being held in the Tower, the crew were being forced upon me against my will, and Smythe, for all his bluster about the great things we should achieve, scrimped and saved on the supply. I was disheartened and much in need of an ally."

"You had me," Bylot said, hurt that his friend had not approached him with his worries.

"You were as busy as I with the preparations. I did not wish to burden you more. In any case, Greene presented himself, full of honeyed words and, despite being an obvious landsman, well versed in the lore of geography and the sea. He also undertook many kindnesses for Katherine that would make her wait much more pleasant. Greene was a godsend at a moment when I desperately needed one.

"I see now that he is not the paragon I thought and wished for. He is as one of those strange creatures I have heard tell of in the tropical zones, that changes their colour to suit their background. Greene can be a skryer to Dee, a considerate friend to Katherine, and who knows what else? But his real purpose in insinuating himself onto the voyage escapes me. To what end is he Dee's creature?"

"I do not know," Bylot lied.

"Are you certain of that master mate?"

A chill ran down Bylot's spine. "What do you mean?"

"Come, come," Hudson said with a smile. "There is more to you than meets the eye. You are a good friend and companion, but you know much of lost journals and ancient maps. Do you voyage only for yourself, or do Dee or Smythe have their claws in you?"

Bylot's instinctive reaction was to deny, but Hudson's smile undermined him. He had already committed to supporting Hudson. Was it not better to cast his lot completely with Hudson than either of the would-be puppet masters? Here was his chance to simplify life, to throw off the murky doings of the world back in London and lose himself in the service of this honourable man on these shores where even existence itself was simple—live or die. A weight lifted from Bylot's shoulders. "I was approached by both."

"Indeed." Hudson raised an eyebrow in mild surprise. "And whom did you choose?"

"Both," Bylot said returning Hudson's smile. "I am both Smythe's agent and Dee's errand boy."

Hudson nodded. "I suspect you are not the only tentacle

Smythe has wrapped around our venture, but what errand do you run for the Magus?"

"He charged me with the collection of one of the four prime elements from a mystical point hereabouts."

"And have you fulfilled that commitment to Dee?"

"Not yet. I am to collect a vial of water from a place where a river flows into the bay before three rounded hills. I believe it to be close by, a little to the west."

"So you wish to continue our westerly course as well?"

"No flask of water, however mystical, is worth a man's life."

Hudson smiled weakly. "To what purpose does Dee require this element?"

"Dee wishes examples of all four elements collected from certain cardinal points that the alchemists believe hold magic powers. All four together will allow him great power, as he believes, to recreate the Golden Age of Troy. Earth and air he collected himself. Fire was my task on poor Davis's final voyage, and now I seek the last."

"I see at least *your* purpose. Dee's is, as ever, shrouded. So, the collection of this element will fulfill your obligation to Dee?"

"It will."

"Good. And if this were, in part, also Greene's purpose here, it would explain his withholding of the map until we were close to Dee's location. Is that his only interest?"

"I cannot say if it is his only purpose, but it is certainly one."

Hudson nodded agreement. "Thank you for your honesty, Robert. It is a freshening breeze in this bucket of lies and deceit. Since there is now naught between us, I ask once more, will you consent to be my man and aid me in the fulfillment of my task?"

"As far as I am able."

"Then take the coat. I will attend to the difficulties."

Reluctantly, Bylot took the coat and stood.

"As to our decisions, they are not pressing. Our choices are limited by circumstance and we must make do as best we can. We will settle the complexities come the spring. Thank you again, Robert."

$$\Psi$$

The winter in Michaelmass Bay was hard. Little stood out from the background of cold, boredom, pain and misery. As far as Bylot could tell, Greene held his peace at Hudson's decision over the coat, but the man became sullen and became even closer to Juet. The pair, often in company with William Wilson, had considerable success over the winter hunting fowl. It was in the spring that the birds left and the aching joints and black lips of scurvy appeared among the crew. Thomas Wydehouse created a potion of pine seeds that tasted like turpentine but eased many pains. Unfortunately, many seeds were required and some men could not stomach the foul liquid.

There were endless days as the light increased and the weather warmed, and Bylot and the others waited desperately for some sign that the ice was preparing to release them. Although it creaked and groaned at all hours, no open water showed until May, and then only in narrow cracks that quickly closed. The bitter wind whistling off the bay was constant and Bylot suspected it was forcing the ice onto their shore. Perhaps had they camped upon the western shore, they would have been released the sooner, but it was fruitless to dwell on might-have-beens.

The crew seemed trapped on some cruel wheel of fate. No sooner did something occur that offered hope and relief—a good catch of fish or a visit from a savage who promised trade—then all their hopes were dashed. The fish disappeared from the bay and the savage never returned. All through the spring they alternated between hope and despair. Even in June, when they at last ventured forth from their anchorage into open water, it proved but a transitory thing and they were almost immediately trapped again in the ice.

None aboard had the resilience to throw off discouragement. Bylot suspected that much of the misery amongst the crew was due to their pitiful diet of mouldy biscuits and stale cheese, enlivened only by the occasional bony fish. It did starve their bodies, but perhaps it starved their souls as much.

And, despite Bylot's pleadings, Hudson seemed bent on encouraging the crew's fears. When all craved a clear goal to which they could bend what will and strength remained, he vacillated. To some he intimated that home was their goal; to others, Cathay. To Bylot he explained that a policy of uncertainty would prevent a conspiracy solidifying against him. He was not swayed when Bylot pointed out that it also prevented a solidifying of any support.

"Ship's commander is a lonely position," Hudson said as the pair talked after the noon sightings on June 20. "All must be mine for good or ill."

"Is our true goal still Cathay this year?"

"With a fair wind and good leads through the ice, we will reach the top of Michaelmass Bay this day and I plan to set course west."

"We have but fourteen days' food on hand."

"Then it matters not where we go. Luck must find us food on any course, else we starve. Do you not wish to visit Dee's mystical point?"

"For a safe conclusion to our venture, I shall fill Dee's vial with good Thames water and swear it is the most magical concoction on earth."

Hudson laughed. "Well said, my one true friend. But, for the moment, the ice forces us to the west and we but follow the leads as they open. Not even the greatest desire to head home can melt ice before its time."

"True enough, but I hope the crew see it thus. They are sick and tired and do not see the world as a rational place."

"In that, at least, they are correct. Do not worry so, Robert. Come high summer, we shall have a hold filled with the jewels of Cathay and the spices of the Moluccas. Then we need worry only about the weight of our fortune dragging us down."

Bylot laughed dutifully at Hudson's frivolity, but nothing could dispel the sense of impending doom growing in his belly.

# 12

## Mutiny

I ce pans glistened in the low sun as Bylot stood the morning watch in the cold spring air of June 22. They were sailing west at last, along a wide, open stretch of water between a low-lying, fog-wreathed coastline to the south and a solid barrier of ice to the north. No one had complained too loudly about the decision, mostly, Bylot assumed, because any other course was impossible due to the ice.

As Bylot mused on their uncertain future, he became aware of activity on deck. Greene and William Wilson were deep in conversation beside the foremast and Juet was headed for the Great Cabin.

"What goes on?" Bylot asked Juet as he passed.

Juet flashed a sly look. "'Tis naught of your business, Master Bylot. Attend to the ship."

Before he could question Juet further, the man ducked into the great cabin. He emerged a short while later to summon Greene, who joined him in Hudson's domain.

Bylot puzzled over what the meeting might mean. He had determined that he would leave his post and find some excuse to intrude when Clements called down from the crow's nest, "Land ahead!"

It could mean only one thing, but Bylot asked nonetheless. "Which way does she head?"

"Northward."

"And is there a way through the ice?"

"There seems not."

"Very well. Keep an eye out.

"Master Jack." Bylot called Hudson's son, who had been hovering at the rail, forward. "Pray interrupt your father with the news that land lies ahead, trending north to south and that there appears no way through."

"Aye, aye," the boy responded seriously.

As Bylot waited for orders, he pondered on this new development. Was it but a minor inconvenience or the end of Hudson's dream? How would the crew react to either?

Bylot's thoughts were interrupted by John Hudson's return. The boy looked puzzled. "We are to come about."

So it was retreat. "Bring her about, Master Mowter," Bylot instructed the boatswain's mate at the helm. The ship heeled over as she swung around and caught the wind. At least the journey east would be with a good following wind. They would return to Michaelmass Bay in but a few short hours. But what did that mean?

Bylot noticed that John Hudson was still hovering by his side. "What ails you, Jack?"

"Why are we giving up?" The boy was near tears. "Father said we were so close and that a few more days would see us succeed. Surely that land ahead is but a promontory."

Bylot was trying to think of something comforting to say to John when Juet and Greene burst out of the Great Cabin, with Juet bleeding profusely from his nose. As they passed, Juet hissed, "We would speak with you Master Bylot."

"I do not take orders from you," Bylot said. "Hold this course," he instructed Mowter and headed for the great cabin.

Bylot knocked and entered to find Hudson sitting at his table. He was hunched over some papers and looked years older than when Bylot had last seen him. "Ah, Robert. I was about to send for you."

"We have come about as you ordered and make good time eastward."

"Good. Good," Hudson said distractedly. "I have a favour to ask of you."

"Anything."

Hudson stood shakily and handed Bylot a leather-bound book. "This is my journal. I have written my life within this volume—my hopes, my fears and my dreams. I intended it, as I began, as a story for John, so that he might understand his father, but now I fear it might be my sole testament. Will you keep it safe for me?"

"Certainly. But why can you not keep it with your charts and papers?"

"I fear these are uncertain times. You will stand by me, Robert?"

"Of course."

"Good. Then that is myself, you, John, Staffe and King. Five of twenty-two."

"There are others."

"Yes, Ludlowe, Butte, Wydehouse, perhaps even Moore and Fanner, but they are a sickly lot, scarce able to rise from their beds."

"Why do you count us so? What did Juet and Greene threaten?"

"Oh, naught. I but wonder who my friends are." Hudson's gaze wandered distractedly around the cabin.

"We are to return by the Overfall then?" Bylot asked.

"I fear none shall return by any route."

Bylot was about to argue when he noticed the map lying open on the table. He recognized the lines of Greene's copied fragment, but this one looked different—older.

"What is that?" he asked, stepping forward.

Hudson roused himself and pulled other charts over top. "'Tis but an old map. Do not concern yourself. Will you call the men to the mast? We shall determine our fate."

Bylot hesitated. "Is it wise to put this to a vote?"

"It is too late for votes. Please do as I ask, Robert. And keep the journal safe."

"I shall."

Bylot stuffed the journal inside his cloak and pushed past Staffe who stood by the mizzen mast at the door to the tool room. As he crossed the deck, deep in confused thoughts, he was approached by Juet. "Again I ask you for a word, Master Bylot."

"I have not the time for your idle chatter, Juet."

"You shall find my chatter much to your benefit, I can assure you. The next few minutes may save your life, and many others."

Juet led Bylot forward into the gunroom where Greene and John Thomas waited.

"What mischief do you have planned?" Bylot asked.

"No mischief, Robert," Greene said in his silkiest voice. "We are simply of the mind that something needs be done or we shall all perish."

"And you think mutiny is what needs be done?"

"I would not call it mutiny, but self-preservation."

"And what will they call it back in London when you swing from the end of a rope?"

"It will be a moot point if we do not return," Juet interrupted. "Time is short and you must make a decision, Master Bylot. We plan this day on taking over the *Discovery* and sailing for home. We—"

"The decision for home is already made."

"Let me finish!" Juet ordered. "We invoke the rule of the sea, whereby some needs be sacrificed for the survival of the rest."

"And you will not be one to be sacrificed."

The speed of Juet's blow caught Bylot unawares. He saw the flash of fist and felt a ringing blow on the side of his head. The force knocked him against the wall. Thomas stepped forward threateningly and Bylot noticed for the first time that he carried a sword.

"I shall speak," Juet snapped, "or you will be the first sacrificed."

"Juet, Juet." Greene said soothingly. "Keep your heat in control. We would not go off before our time."

Bylot massaged the growing lump on the side of his head. His ears were ringing, but everything appeared remarkably clear. He could hear the tap of Thomas's sword point as he drummed it monotonously on the deck and smell the sweat of fear coming from Juet, but just as at the skrying, it was Greene's voice that commanded his attention.

"Now, Master Bylot, it sits thus. Wydehouse, Moore and the lame Fanner are like to die ere we reach the Overfall, and Ludlowe, Butte, Clement and Bond are not far removed. They eat our precious supplies to no end and must be put out. Hudson will not allow this, therefore he and his brat must also go. Of the rest, Staffe and King are Hudson's men through, but the remainder will do as we please to live. What of you?"

"I am Hudson's man also," Bylot said, struggling to keep his voice firm and his fear hidden. "I shall not countenance this villainy. You shall all hang if I live to tell of this."

"Well spoken," Greene said with a smile. "Now that your sentiments are out in the open, think on this, and think well. John Thomas here would as happy as not run his sword through you on a word from me." Bylot glanced at Thomas, whose grin convinced him of the truth of what Greene said. "In that case, you would die to no purpose. We are certain of success and can cast the dead adrift as easily as the living.

"In the truth of it, your skills in navigation would be much beneficial to those who live on. You may not care a jot for myself, Juet, William Wilson or Thomas, but think on the others—Surgeon Wilson, Adrian Mowter, Abacuk Prickett, Bennett Mathew, Nicholas Simmes. They be not strong in with us. Would you see them condemned as well for want of an able navigator? Your choice is to end your own life here or, perhaps, save the lives of others. I swear, none of them will be implicated on our return, regardless of whether Juet and I swing. Think on it, but not too long."

The journal beneath Bylot's cloak weighed heavy. He had a responsibility to protect that, which precluded an immediate attack on Juet and Greene—not that that offered any chance of success with Thomas fingering his sword eagerly in the background. If he could get to his chest, he could break the alchemist's globe and release its power. But he was too afraid, both of its unknown power and of Thomas's sword.

Verbal persuasion was equally likely to fail. That would lead only to him being locked away, or worse—navigational skills be damned. Bylot allowed himself a small smile. It wasn't his ability to steer a ship that the mutineers needed. No, Juet was capable of that. Bylot knew why he was being offered a place on the voyage home. There were probably two reasons Bylot was being approached now.

If he agreed to this plan, his lot would be inextricably linked to the leaders of the mutiny. He had a perceived standing with Smythe and Dee, and to the authorities in London that would far outweighed Juet or Greene's. Bylot's presence when they returned home would greatly increase their chances of avoiding the hangman.

On a more practical note, Bylot was one of the few able-bodied men who was capable of fighting for Hudson. If Staffe, King, Hudson and Bylot organized against the mutiny, they stood some chance of success. But that wouldn't happen now, Bylot was neutralized whatever he decided. Unless he wanted to die bloodily here in this room, he had little real choice. Perhaps a chance would come later to influence events? At least, he rationalized, if he protected the journal the true story could be told.

"Come on. We have not all day," Juet snarled. Thomas stepped forward.

"Very well," Bylot said. "It seems I have little choice. I will not stand in your way. But I shall countenance no bloodshed. Those to be set adrift shall not be harmed and shall be allowed to take whatever goods they wish to aid them in the wilderness."

"Agreed," Greene said. "Now to the oath taking."

"Oath taking?"

"We must be bound to this thing," Greene said. "John Thomas, you first."

Thomas stepped forward, holding his blade by his side. "You shall swear truth to God," Greene intoned, "your prince and country: You shall do nothing but to the glory of God and the good of the action in hand."

"I shall," Thomas declared.

"And not harm any man," Bylot added.

Thomas looked at Greene who nodded. "I shall."

"Good. Now, John, fetch the rest of our party while I see to Master Bylot."

Bylot swallowed hard and agreed to the oath. One by one, the other mutineers and some of the neutral men filed in—either willingly or under threat of death—to be bound by the oath: William Wilson, Michael Perce, Francis Clements, Adrian Mowter, Abacuk Prickett, Sylvanus Bond and Nicholas Simmes. Bylot was surprised at the number. Greene and Juet had prepared well.

"The surgeon and the cook refuse to swear," Juet said, "but they will not stand against us and we will have need of them on the journey home."

"And the carpenter," Greene added, "although I fear he will refuse. Now, let us to business. All we ask of you, Master

Bylot, is that you stand to one side. One of us shall be close by, so do not think to change your mind."

Juet and Greene left the gunroom, closing the door after.

Bylot hurriedly opened his cloak and took out the journal. He tucked it beneath his belt, where it felt awkward but left his hands free if need be, and replaced his cloak. Then he opened the door and moved to a shadowy corner where he could watch the deck.

Toward the stern, Greene and Mowter were talking with Staffe while Thomas, William Wilson and Perce lounged nearby. At the watch bell, the door to the great cabin opened and Hudson stepped into the morning light. He was wearing his fur-collared coat and, as was his habit, looked first to the sky to observe the weather. This gave the mutineers their chance. Thomas and Perce stepped smartly forward and clasped Hudson's arms while Wilson bound his wrists together behind him.

"What means this?" Hudson yelled.

"You shall know in the shallop," Wilson replied.

Bylot expected Hudson to berate the men who had laid hands upon him, accusing them of mutiny and threatening the hangman upon their return. Instead, he stood silent, bowed down as if a great weight were pushing him to the deck. For all Hudson's mood swings over the past months, Bylot was surprised by his lack of spirit. He appeared a beaten man before the battle had even begun.

"What villainy is this?" Staffe began, but he was silenced by the threat of Mowter's dagger at his throat.

"Be still, Phillip," Hudson cautioned. "They but dig their own graves."

"Father!" John Hudson burst from the hatch amidships and raced to the stern. Greene made an attempt to capture him, but he easily evaded the grasping arms and clung to his father. "What is going on? Why are you bound? Let him go."

"Be at peace, John. No one will be hurt. Stay by me."

"Bring the shallop alongside," Greene ordered, "and bring the sick on deck. Where is Juet?"

As if in answer, a loud curse echoed from the hold. There was a clash of metal on metal and Juet's voice came up, "He has a sword, bring me aid."

Greene and Wilson moved to the hatch, but were stopped by a strangled scream. John King emerged, holding a bloody sword before him. He was followed by Juet, who pawed uselessly at a stream of blood running from his chest, took two steps and collapsed.

"Release the captain," King ordered, taking in the scene at a glance. When no one moved, he took a step toward Greene, holding his blade ahead. "This is your doing. I knew the mistake Master Hudson made as soon as you stepped aboard in your fancy clothes at Gravesend, and you have done naught to change my opinion since. Now order your minions to release the captain or you will end like that rat, Juet."

It seemed to Bylot that they were part of a tableau carved in stone, every limb so heavy that the effort of movement was too great. The only life in the scene was the dying Juet, who lay twitching and gurgling in a surprisingly large and growing pool of his own blood.

Eventually, Greene broke the silence in his smooth mesmerizing voice. "Master King, there is no need for such haste and harshness. We are all reasonable men here and can resolve this issue to all our satisfactions. The prime agent of our situation lies near death at your feet. For the rest, we can talk. Let us have no more killing. Come, put down your sword and we can resolve this unpleasantness."

King appeared suddenly uncertain. Bylot wanted to shout out to take care, to not trust Greene's honeyed words, but he kept silent. King's sword tip wavered. It was the moment for which Prickett had been waiting. Unobserved, he had been sneaking closer to King, hidden by the capstan, buckets and piles of coiled rope. Now, clutching the short dagger he was never without, he leaped.

King heard him coming and turned, but Prickett easily avoided the clumsy sweep of the sword, clutched one arm around King's shoulders and, with the other, drove the dagger up beneath King's chin and deep into his brain. The sword fell and, without a word, King slumped like a broken doll onto the deck, where his blood mixed with Juet's.

"Damn you, Greene," Bylot found his voice at last. "You promised no bloodshed."

"Then take up your point with Master King. I did not begin this. But enough debating. Does anyone else challenge these doings?"

"You shall all hang," Staffe said.

"Mayhap, but there are many miles 'tween us and the noose. You are welcome to share them with us, Master Staffe. We may have need of your talents."

"I shall take my chances with honest men, if you will let me take my chest."

"Very well, but be quick."

Staffe disappeared toward the tool room and the rest brought the shallop alongside. Bylot made no move to help, but watched in silence as the sick were brought from their beds. Fanner could walk with support, but Ludlowe and Wydehouse were dragged unceremoniously across the deck. All three were dropped, none too gently, into the waiting shallop. Moore and Butte were extremely weak, but managed to clamber down the ropes into the boat.

When Clements was brought up, Thomas stepped toward Greene and pleaded for his friend to stay. Mathew then repeated the same for Bond, claiming that his cooperage talents would be useful when they wished to store any food they caught. Greene reluctantly agreed.

Ludlowe and Butte both behaved poorly, pleading and begging to be allowed back on board, but neither had strong friends among the mutineers and remained in the shallop. Then Hudson, with John walking beside him, joined them. John tried his best to put a brave face on his plight, but he was obviously terrified. Tears welled in his eyes and he made short, choking sounds in his throat as he climbed over the rail.

Hudson walked over the bloodstained deck with his gaze fixed firmly before him. Bylot steeled himself for an outburst of anger as his friend passed by, but it never came. As Hudson drew level, he simply raised his head, looked at Bylot and smiled. It was a thousand times worse than any hurled curse and Bylot had to swallow hard to stop himself crying out.

Finally, Staffe reappeared, dragging his sea chest and with his musket over his shoulder.

"You cannot take the musket," Wilson said as he passed.

Greene held up his hand. "Let him be. They will have need of it, I think."

As Staffe drew level with Bylot, he said, "We will follow you. Leave us a token at the place where the fowls breed on the cape at the Overfall, so we may know you have gone before."

"And if you cannot get that far in the shallop," Bylot said, "I swear I shall return to this place to get you."

Staffe nodded. Bylot could not meet the carpenter's eye. He felt like nothing when faced with such a brave man. Why couldn't he do the honourable thing and climb into the shallop with his friends? Was it really the journal that dug into his back, or was that just a rationale for his fear? Bylot stepped forward to the rail and peered over. He felt the journal shift against his body and angled his hip awkwardly to help keep it in place.

Below him, in the shallop, Hudson sat looking small and beaten. Huddled beside him, and finally letting his tears flow, sat John. The other six sat or lay about. Only Staffe looked back defiantly. He was in the stern, right arm draped over the rudder looking up at those on deck with disdain. William Wilson stood beside Bylot, shouting down in his coarse dialect.

"This shall teach ye the price of hoarding food from honest sailors, Master Henry Hudson."

"There be few enough honest men on this voyage and none are left aboard the ship," Staffe cried a response. "You shall find no hoarded food, but the end of a rope if you survive to return home. It's the gallows for all and I wish you a long drop."

"Damn you Staffe," Wilson began, but he got no farther. In his agitation, he pushed against Bylot, who stumbled. The journal slipped from his belt and fell from beneath his cloak onto the deck.

"What be this?" asked Wilson, bending to retrieve it. "By God's eyes, 'tis a second collection of lies. Were ye bent upon the preservation of this document, Bylot?"

Bylot remained silent. Wilson thrust the book under his nose. "Methinks ye were, and this would hang us for sure. There be room for one more in the shallop." Wilson grabbed Bylot's arm roughly and pushed him toward the ladder.

"Hold!" A soft voice cut across the commotion. Henry Greene stepped forward. "Mayhap you should consider William, that Master Bylot is, with Master Juet's demise, the only navigator on board and thus our greatest chance of escape. Avoiding the gallows will be of no use if we never see home."

"Perchance," Wilson replied, "but he is most certainly in league with Hudson and might see us up the gallows steps if he survives."

"I think not," said Greene. "Master Bylot, will you speak against your shipmates when we return?"

Bylot glanced down at the shallop with its dejected crew and then out over the blue waters with the almost painfully white patches of ice scattered about. They had no food, no charts, no tools, and precious little else aside from the clothes they wore. He did not wish to join them.

"No," he whispered.

"What?"

"No!"

"Good." Greene took the book from Wilson and passed it to Bylot. "Then be so kind as to return this to its rightful owner."

Bylot hesitated. Hudson had placed his trust in him. This would be a huge betrayal. But what choice did he have? He could stand on his principles and join the others in the shallop, or he could survive. If he did the latter, at least there was a chance that the truth of their adventures would be heard.

"Damn you, Henry Greene," Bylot hissed.

Painfully slowly, he held the journal over the rail and let it fall. The pages fluttered almost regretfully in the cold breeze and the book landed with a thump beside Hudson. The noise seemed to start him from his reverie and he glanced at the open journal, then up at Bylot. Again, there was no accusation, just a sadness that Bylot could not bear. He slumped onto the deck with his back to the rail.

"Cut them loose," Greene ordered.

As the shallop drifted to stern, the crew began ransacking the *Discovery* for hoards of food. Greene made no attempt to prevent the destruction other than to say that no one was to enter the great cabin. He also ordered the mainsails hauled in to cut the vessel's speed while there were few to care for its running.

The bodies of King and Juet were unceremoniously dumped over the side. No one bothered to clean the considerable stain of blood that was left to dry in the weak sun.

With a cry of triumph, Thomas announced that he had discovered a cask of beer, the contents of which were soon distributed amongst the mutineers. Other than the beer, however, the fabled hoard of food consisted of little more than some peas, a few pieces of salt pork, some rounds of cheese and two hundred mouldy biscuits, all of which were hurriedly eaten.

Greene took no part in the ransacking, preferring to stand at the rudder. He ordered a reluctant Sylvanus Bond to the crow's nest to keep lookout and called Bylot and Prickett to him.

Bylot hauled himself to his feet and shuffled over. "Are you satisfied?" he asked.

"Satisfied?" Greene said with a smile. "No. I shall be satisfied when we tie up at St. Katherine's Pool."

"And you think this rabble will get us there? Look, they think nothing for the future and simply gorge on whatever comes to hand."

"True enough, but a few biscuits and some rotting pork will add but a day or two to our misery should we not find fresh food at the capes. Let them enjoy the moment—the rest of us have work to do. Master Bylot, you are ship's mate and, with Juet gone, the responsibility for seeing the ship home falls squarely upon you."

Bylot grunted acquiescence. He knew the job he would have to do. It would not be easy and it was a cruel cost for pursuing his dreams.

"Master Prickett," Greene continued. "Your skill with the blade notwithstanding, you have some talents with the quill. You shall take the ship's log and destroy the incriminating sections. Then, I charge you, write a new account of our voyage more suited to our survival. Stay with the truth where it is neutral, but put what you must in our favour."

"I shall," Prickett replied.

"Good. Now go to the great cabin and see to Hudson's papers and charts in preparation for your tasks."

Despite himself, Bylot's heart leapt at the order. Now he would have a chance to study the portolan he had glimpsed on Hudson's table. Bylot led Prickett to the great cabin.

Once inside, the pair were protected from the noise of the looting and destruction overwhelming the rest of the ship. Prickett made for the small book by Hudson's bunk and began thumbing through the ship's log and journal.

"It must all go," he mumbled to himself. "I must rewrite it all."

Bylot rummaged through the papers on the table. There were pages of rough notes and detailed maps of Michaelmass Bay and other islands they had visited. Even Greene's copy of the portolan was there, but the main chart—and the much older map that Bylot was convinced he had glimpsed—were missing. In a rising panic, Bylot tore open the chart drawer. Desperately, he flung out the old maps of Mercator, Plancius and the others. They were too old—or not old enough. He tore open Hudson's chest and flung the contents out. There was no sign of the map he sought. Had he imagined it? How could it have vanished without trace? It *had* been in the great cabin, hadn't it? But it wasn't there now and Hudson had not had a chance to remove it. Who else had been here?

Staffe! He had come back for his trunk and tools. It would have been easy for him to grab the master chart and the portolan and hide them amongst his things. Bylot laughed aloud. They had been tricked.

"What amuses you so?" Prickett asked.

"Naught. I must talk with Greene."

Bylot was halfway across the deck when Bond called from the crow's nest, "The shallop draws near."

Bylot joined the rush to the aft rail. The shallop had its single sail raised and was bearing down on the *Discovery*. Staffe sat in the stern, manipulating the rudder, and John Hudson sat in the bow, like a carved figurehead. All on board the *Discovery* watched in awe as if they were seeing ghosts.

A loud crack broke the silence. Bylot looked over to see Thomas standing with a smoking musket in his hand. The range was too far for anything but the luckiest shot to have any effect, but Greene berated Thomas and demanded that no more violence be offered the shallop's crew. Then he ordered the sails unfurled, and the gap slowly began to widen. John Hudson slumped back into the shallop. Phillip Staffe shook his fist and shouted something, but his words were lost in the snap of the *Discovery*'s sails and the creak of her straining timbers.

The crew returned to their pillage, but Bylot stood alone at the rail until the shallop disappeared from sight. He was encouraged by the way it was being handled and convinced himself that the occupants had a chance to follow the *Discovery* through the Overfall and, at the least, find succour with fishermen on the New Founde Land coast.

Bylot turned his gaze to the distant land. The early-morning fog had burned off and the air was clear. The land lay only a few miles off. It was low lying for the most part, and a medium-sized river brought a mix of brown mud and silt to discolour the sea. Bylot was too lost in his misery to recognize immediately what he was looking at. Beside the river mouth, three low hills broke the flat horizon—Dee's location. The fourth element was there to be collected.

"Are the charts in order, Master Bylot?" Greene stood at Bylot's shoulder.

"Charts—" Bylot stammered, confused by Greene's sudden presence. Had he seen the hills? Should Bylot draw his attention to them?

"Aye, the charts you went to the great cabin to examine."

Bylot had left the cabin in order to tell Greene the charts were missing, but the sight of the shallop and its forlorn crew had changed his mind. Their need of the main chart was more pressing than his—Bylot could navigate from the readings in the ship's official log before Prickett destroyed it. But what of the portolan? It would be impossible to rescue it without depriving the shallop of the chart, and yet it was probably the most valuable map in existence anywhere in the world.

"Do not dwell on their fate," Greene said, waving an arm dismissively at the receding shallop. "They brought it on themselves. We must look to our fate. Are the charts in order?"

Bylot thought about the portolan. Certainly, it was invaluable and he would love to see it, but it had cost men's lives. If Hudson and Staffe made it safe home, the portolan would be put about for all to see. If Greene took it back, it would remain secret. If it stayed with Staffe and the crew of the shallop did not survive, neither would the ancient map. Which was best?

"Yes," Bylot said, turning from the rail, "the charts are in order."

"Good." Greene turned and strode forward. Bylot did not call him back and point out the three hills. Dee could do his magic without his help.

# 13

## Returns

B ylot did the absolute minimum on the voyage home. Each day, if the sky was clear, he took readings and plotted their course on a makeshift chart that he constructed from patching together small maps he found in the great cabin. The navigational calculations stretched his learning to the limit and took up most of his waking time. Still, in whatever free time he did have, he took no part in the activities of the ship, preferring to stand aside and watch the mutineers squabble among themselves. In truth, Bylot cared very little what happened to him and worked on the navigation only to save the crew members who had taken no part in the mutiny.

When they reached Digges Cape, Greene insisted that a party go ashore to hunt birds or steal them from the caches that the local peoples had laid aside. He told Bylot to lead the party, but Bylot refused—there was nothing Greene could do to force him. As sole navigator, Bylot was too valuable to cast adrift. Eventually, Greene led the party, consisting of Thomas, Perce and William Wilson, ashore.

The shore party had been gone for several hours. Bylot and the others lounged on the deck in the sun, conserving energy. Bylot was dozing off and half-dreaming of a sumptuous, steaming bowl of venison stew when he was roused by a distant commotion.

Peering over the ship's rail, Bylot saw the longboat near the shore. It was being rowed by Greene and Wilson while Perce pushed it out of the shallow water. All three men were yelling at the tops of their voices. Bylot barely had time to wonder where Thomas was when he appeared round an outcrop of rock on the shore, chased by about a dozen screaming tribesmen.

Thomas never stood a chance. Long before he reached the water's edge, he had fallen, six long, feathered shafts sticking out of his back.

"They'll never make it," Bennett Mathew voiced Bylot's thoughts as the tribesmen ignored Thomas's twitching body and splashed into the shallows.

"Get the muskets," Mathew shouted.

A couple of men did as they were told, but the rest simply stood along the rail and watched in horrified fascination.

Greene and Wilson were rowing as hard as they could and Perce was vainly trying to scramble into the boat. He almost made it a couple of times, but Greene and Wilson refused to slow to allow him to scramble aboard and, at last, Perce slipped and the longboat surged away from him.

The attackers were only about ten feet from Perce when he regained his footing. Screaming for help, he tried to run through the waist-deep water, but the first axe caught him on the side of the head and he went down. A flurry of blows turned the water a frothy red and Perce disappeared.

"My God," Mathew said, "they abandoned him."

Realizing that they couldn't catch the boat, the attackers launched a flight of arrows toward the escaping men. One sank deep into Greene's shoulder and another pierced

Wilson's neck. The longboat slewed around wildly, but Greene managed to push Wilson aside and regain control. Slowly the boat neared the *Discovery*.

When they were finally pulled aboard, both men were covered in blood. Greene was cursing loudly as he struggled to pull the arrow out of his shoulder. Wilson, with an arrow sticking out both sides of his neck, could make only strange choking noises as the blood bubbled from his mouth. Several men, led by Mathew, hurried to help their companions.

"Leave them," Bylot ordered.

"But ..." Mathew began.

Bylot gave him no chance to speak. "Leave them and raise the sails, or we will soon join them." He pointed back at the shore where several light canoes had been launched and were speeding toward them.

The crew needed no further encouragement. As the wounded men lay bleeding, the two loaded muskets were discharged to discourage the pursuers and the sails raised; the *Discovery* drew away.

Greene eventually managed to remove the arrow from his shoulder so he could begin to heal, but Wilson was doomed.

Bylot found himself completely unmoved by the grisly fate of his companions. He continued to navigate, but kept to himself. Effectively, he was captain, but he couldn't bring himself to occupy the great cabin. He took over Staffe's old bunk in the gunroom and retreated there at every opportunity.

Fair winds favoured the *Discovery* the entire way across the Atlantic. This was fortunate since the slightest delay would have meant the death of the entire crew. As it was, they survived by eating feathers and candle grease and were so close to death that the Irish fishermen who discovered them drifting off the coast recoiled in horror at the sight.

The eight survivors were taken to London to have their fate decided. On the journey, much of the crew deliberated endlessly on their chances of avoiding the hangman's noose, putting great faith in John Dee's ability to sway opinion. When they arrived in London, however, they learned that the seemingly immortal Magus had died of the fever around the time they had been starving in Michaelmass Bay. Bylot took no part in the speculation. He didn't care what happened to him.

The survivors were taken to Marshalsea Prison where, after regaining their strength, they were all required to write an account of the voyage. Bylot refused as, to his surprise, did Greene. At last, they were brought before their employer, Thomas Smythe.

"The call for your death is universal," Smythe opened by saying. "Henry Hudson was a well-respected man with many friends in the city. You revolted against your ship's master and cast him and eight other poor souls adrift to die a most horrible death. It is a question only of a swift trial and a public noose.

"True, Prickett's journal and many of your individual accounts apportion the lion's share of blame for the insurrection to those who conveniently died on the return journey. But this does not alter your state. The law is certain. On-board ship, the captain is God and to stand against him is death."

Several of the men groaned out loud at Smythe's words. Edward Wilson and Sylvanus Bond fell to their knees and began praying loudly.

Bylot stood aside, a disinterested observer, reflecting on

man's need to strive for life, however doomed the attempt might be. Smythe had already turned to leave when Greene stepped forward and spoke. He was the main surviving mutineer and deserved above all others to hang.

"You cannot send us to the hangman," he said boldly.

All conversation ceased. Smythe stared hard at Greene who had a half-smile on his thin lips.

"Well, Master Greene," Smythe said, "From what I understand, you are the one most in need of hanging. I am a man of business, however, and I do agree there's little profit in stretching your necks, but 'cannot'? The law is clear and I am not above that."

"But the king is."

"You would call His Majesty into this? What arrogant presumption causes you to think he will take an interest in the sad doings of some ragged mutineers?"

"The prosperity and security of the nation," Greene said calmly. "These men you see in this room hold upon their shoulders the most valuable heads in England. To extinguish the flame of reason that burns within each would be a calumny of the first order."

All eyes, including Bylot's, were now fixed on Greene. Bylot knew Greene to be almost as expert a manipulator as Smythe himself. There was a spark of interest in who might win this confrontation.

"What nonsense do you speak?" Smythe asked. "You are but a rabble of mutineers led by a villain who owes allegiance to a dead mystic. I would regret Master Bylot's end, he had some promise as a navigator, and I might warrant that you had some cause for your actions but that is

215

no concern of the king. Speak plainly or it shall be the worse for you."

"The worse for men about to be hanged?" Greene asked sarcastically. He continued before Smythe had time to express an indignant reply. "Henry Hudson was correct. The Furious Overfall does lead to the shores of Cathay."

Bylot gasped involuntarily. Hudson was dead or dying because the mutineers, Greene among them, had not believed they were on the verge of breaking through to the Pacific Ocean. All had seen the shore trending north before they turned back.

"You have in this room," Greene went on, "men who, in the matter of the Northwest Passage to Cathay, are more versed than Frobisher, Davis or even Drake himself. We have traversed the Furious Overfall, a feat none other has accomplished. These men before you have felt waves from Cathay lift the hull beneath their feet. They have smelled air perfumed with the odour of spices. No others have achieved so much, nor could yet achieve so much more again."

"Why then did you not achieve your glorious goals last year?"

"Because men are weak and flawed. They fear the unknown and, without a Columbus or Drake to lead them, they doubt the possibilities. Juet doubted and Hudson was no Drake."

"So you say you were within an ace of glory, but weakness on the part of those conveniently silent prevented?"

"Not within an ace," Greene said smoothly. "Henry Hudson was no Drake at the figures either. He thought to be within a few days' sail of Drake's Nova Albion. In truth he had much farther to go. Too far, with the sickness and starvation we had."

Bylot and the others watched Greene's performance in silence. It was a masterful blending of fact, half-truth and lie, but it seemed to be building an edifice that was intriguing Smythe.

"And what makes you think I, or the king, should believe that you would do better next season?" Smythe asked.

"Three things. First," Greene began counting off on his fingers, "we know our mistake. It was in turning south when we exited the Furious Overfall. That enmeshed us in the bays and islands of a barren coast, trapped us too late in the year and forced us to endure a winter that caused many of our woes.

"Had we but set course west, we should have discovered the outlet we sought or, at least, have come upon the northernmost coast of the Americas far enough on that to round the northwest cape would have been a matter of some ease."

Smythe nodded thoughtfully as Greene checked a second finger.

"A return through the Overfall would be led by an expert and one of the greatest navigators of our age."

"Who?" Smythe asked.

Greene turned to his companions and theatrically threw out a hand. "Robert Bylot."

Bylot was stunned. He began to stammer a response, but Greene held up his hand to silence him.

"Robert Bylot performed admirably as Hudson's mate in those waters. None other who performed that duty yet lives. But what is more, he singlehandedly brought the *Discovery* safe home though the many perils of violent storm and savage attack with a rotten ship and starving, short-handed crew. It was a feat little short of miraculous."

Smythe looked long and hard at Bylot. Bylot wanted to deny the overblown rhetoric, but had no wish to undermine Greene's flow.

"But yet you all saw a coast tending north and closing the bay," Smythe returned his gaze to Greene. "Even the greatest navigator of the age cannot sail a ship over dry land."

"True enough," Greene agreed amicably, "but the land we saw is merely a small peninsula. It would be but a minor deviation to round it."

"How can you know?"

"I know," Greene said, checking off a third finger, "because I have seen a map."

Every head in the room snapped around to stare at Greene who stood calmly. Bylot's mind reeled. A map was the thread that had woven men's greed into a sack that had held only disaster. Bylot thought he had heard the last of the mysterious portolan, but here was Greene bringing it up again.

"A map?" Smythe asked.

"Yes, a portolan—or rather a copy of one—that showed the outlet from the Great Sea at 58 degrees and connecting west to Drake's outlet into the Southern Ocean."

"You have this map?"

"No." Greene managed to put a regretful tone in his voice. "It was in Master Hudson's possession at the end and, although I searched the ship after his abandonment, I could find no trace of it."

"How convenient," Smythe said sarcastically. "Why

should I believe you?"

"Because," Greene's smile broadened, "Master Bylot has seen the map, too."

Now all eyes fixed on Bylot. Calmly, he stared back. He knew the map to which Greene referred. It had to be the copy he had glimpsed on Hudson's chart table. Had it shown a passage? Bylot could not be sure. He had caught a look at a coastline turning north, but had there been a break farther up, at 58 degrees? He had not had the time to see. Not that it mattered now. The truth was irrelevant. If Bylot didn't want his companions to hang, his role was clear.

"I have seen it." Bylot swallowed hard. "It was rough, but it showed an outlet to the northwest of where we wintered in Michaelmass Bay. I believe Henry Greene is correct and that a westerly course from the Furious Overfall would lead a well-handled ship direct toward it."

"And where did this wondrous map originate?"

"It had a long and checkered past," Greene explained, "but ended in the safe hands of Doctor Dee."

"I might have guessed as much," Smythe sneered.

"The Magus gave it into my keeping to encourage Master Hudson should his will fail. I believe that was in parallel with your own wishes?"

Smythe nodded thoughtfully. "I do not trust you, Greene, but you have given me much to think on. I shall ponder further and see what is to be done."

As Smythe left, Greene turned to Bylot and winked. Bylot looked away in confusion. As much as Bylot hated him, Greene had offered him a chance at a life beyond this tragic voyage. But Bylot had accepted the idea of bearing the weight of his guilt to the grave. It was a fair price for betraying a friend. And now this—hope. The guilt was a burden, yes, but did he really want to hang for it? As the door closed behind Smythe, Bylot crouched in a corner and silently damned Greene.

Ψ

Smythe had done much. Not only had he convinced the powers that be to ignore, for the moment, the consequences of mutiny and prevent the men swinging from Tyburn gallows, he had put together funds to refurbish the *Discovery* and finance a voyage the following summer.

The orders were to traverse the Furious Overfall and sail west to round the northwest cape of the Americas before crossing the Pacific. So sure were they of success that Captain Button carried a letter of introduction to the Emperor of Cathay from King James.

A secondary purpose had been to rescue any of Hudson's crew who might have survived, but Smythe made certain that Bylot knew this was just for public consumption. In no way was it to interfere with the main purpose.

Bylot agreed to sail with Button as did Greene, Prickett and Wilson, although, in reality, none had a choice if they wished to live.

Bylot rationalized that he was going to rescue Hudson and the others, but deep inside he knew that was not true. What drove him that winter was the same old dream. What if Greene had told the truth? What if the portolan did show an outlet at 58 degrees? The glittering prize of a short route to Cathay might still be possible! And would that not be what Hudson wanted?

In the months before they sailed, Bylot avoided everyone, particularly Katherine. Although she had been released from the Tower, Bylot could not face her. He had no wish to see Smythe or Greene, and Dee was dead, although the Magus had left a parting gift. One evening as Bylot sat, drowning his misery in wine, a messenger brought him a package. Inside were two books—Trithemius's *Steganographia*. Bylot no longer had any interest in these ancient code books; they were part of a different time—a time when he was filled with expectations and thrilled at what the world had to offer him. He had no idea why Dee had taken the trouble to leave them to him or to write the inscription inside the cover: *"To my young friend, Robert Bylot, who wishes to see Apollo rest only alone. Look backward within the earthly sphere, my friend, and may Uriel and 1,132,221,111,211 angels bless your endeavours. Dee."*

Bylot didn't care about Dee's mystical nonsense. The Golden Age—if there ever had been one—would never be recreated. Everyone had to do the best they could in the world as they found it. Bylot set the books aside and forgot them.

Ψ

On a cold April day in 1612, Bylot's waiting ended. The *Discovery*—the blood of the previous year scrubbed off her decks, the torn sails replaced and the rotten timbers strengthened—sailed once more for the Furious Overfall.

In almost a mockery of the struggles of the previous

summer, the Atlantic crossing and the passage through the Overfall were easily completed. A full day into the Great Sea, Bylot stood in the bow, squinting against the glare of the sun reflecting off the snow that blanketed the ice floes dotting the grey swells. The weather was cold but fair and they were making good time westward.

Bylot's gaze was fixed resolutely forward, to the west. He would not—could not—look south where the same snow might be covering the frozen white corpses of a tiny group of his closest friends.

"Do you not think to turn us south, Master Bylot?" Henry Greene appeared beside Bylot in the bow.

"Captain Button is in command," Bylot replied tersely.

"In name, aye, but you know as well as I that he is merely a figurehead untainted by mutiny and that he will do your bidding. You carry the authority of Smythe and the others."

"And who employs you, Greene, now that your mystical master is dead?" Bylot asked, turning to face the other man.

Greene's thin mouth curled into something resembling a smile. "I look to myself, Master Bylot, as always—and as should we all."

"And that is why you had Prickett create that abominable fiction to replace Master Hudson's true journal?"

"What is truth? This deck beneath our feet is true, as are those waves that march at us from the west. For the rest, I cannot say what will be, and what has been can ne'er be recaptured. As men, we form the world to our needs. Should we treat the past any differently?"

"Where our lies impugn the names of honourable men,

we should."

"Honourable men? Who is honourable? The money-grubbing Smythe? The mystical Dee? The self-serving Juet? Yourself? Honour is a luxury for children's tales and knights.

"You stand here now, pulled to the south where men who believed your promise of a year past may, at this moment, await in hope your arrival. To save them would be honourable, but you will not. You are headed west and will continue so, for that way lies the answer to your dream."

"Look how we suffered one winter," Bylot responded angrily. "No one could survive two. They are all dead. It would be a wild goose chase and a wasted season to sail south."

"But not knowing drives you insane."

Bylot ignored Greene's comment. "Did the map really show an outlet?" He was looking for an answer, pleading for a certainty that he was following the right course.

"Does it matter what the map showed? Everyone, yourself included, wishes to believe it shows what I said it did. Even were I to say now that it showed only an unbroken coast with no way through, no one would believe me. You would dissemble, say I was lying now for my own dark purposes. The philosophers talk of truth, but everyone in this sad tale has sought only the truth they wish. Belief is a much headier brew than truth. You chase honour, but you still sail west. Oh, you will say to yourself that in heading west you are fulfilling Hudson's dream—that it is your duty to reach his goal rather than waste our one chance on a wild goose chase after men who are already dead. But it

will haunt you, Robert Bylot. However much you tell yourself now that Hudson, Staffe and the others had no hope,
should you outlive the sum of Methuselah, you will always
ask yourself, 'Did any live?'" Greene turned and walked
away, leaving Bylot to stare out at the ice, the snow and the
western horizon.

Ψ

After days on open water, they saw land, not trending east
to west as they had hoped, but north to south. They followed the coast north until winter forced them into a river
they named Nelson for the sailing master. Many, including
Nelson, died that awful winter of ship's fever, scurvy and
simple want. The last had been Greene.

Bylot had been beside him as Greene cursed the world
through blackened lips in his final delirium. He talked with
angels in voices Bylot well remembered and died as the
ship was preparing to sail for home. Bylot had shed many
tears for the deaths that haunted his life, but he had none
for Greene. Dee, Bylot thought, had honestly believed in his
dreams of empires and angels. Greene had merely manipulated the world for his own purposes, and men had died
because of it. The mysterious skryer deserved his end.

In the summer of 1613, Bylot led the tattered remnants of
Button's crew around the perimeter of the Great Sea, finally
proving that it was not an open ocean. Then he went home.

But there was no rest for Bylot. He had ignored the
course his conscience had tried to tell him to follow for a
glory that had turned to ashes in his mouth. Even Button's

rationale that the voyage was a success in that it had discovered much, and Bylot's own knowledge that it had saved his neck from being stretched, was no comfort. His low mood was compounded by the honours showered on Button who was knighted, made an admiral and died a wealthy, respected man. Even the Great Sea was known by his name for many years.

Bylot returned north on two more voyages, seeking the other passage shown on the portolan. He failed to find it and instead watched as his discoveries were named for his new captain, William Baffin.

Bylot retreated to his shabby rooms in Wapping. Patiently, he waited for death to release him. It was a long wait.

# EPILOGUE

## THE FINAL ALCHEMY

There was no more time. Bylot had stalled as long as he could—remembered as much from his life as he had stored in his tired brain—now he had to find answers. Not all the answers would be in the book he had purchased from Gilby. Bylot craved to know more of the mysterious portolan, for instance. Had it really existed or was it just one of Greene's schemes. But one answer would be there—the answer to that most important question: "Did any live?"

Answers. That's all we seek, Bylot thought. Even Dee with his crystals and code books—he was just as lost as anyone. Bylot smiled at the thought of all the hours he had wasted translating the different layers of Trithemius's nonsense. His eyes drifted up to the two dusty volumes sitting on the shelf by the fire. He hadn't opened them since he'd first read Dee's cryptic inscription.

"Dear God!" Bylot froze. Understanding hit him like a hammer blow. One answer, at least, had been right in front of him all these years! He knew now why Dee had bequeathed him Trithemius's books. They were a message from a dead man. The books themselves were nonsense, but they were a clue to reading the real message—the inscription.

Bylot struggled to his bookcase and took down the first volume. "To my young friend, Robert Bylot, who wishes to see Apollo rest only alone. Look backward within the earthly sphere, my friend, and may Uriel and 1,132,221,111,211 angels bless your endeavours. Dee."

What did Bylot wish to see? "Apollo rest only alone." Nineteen letters. He added up the numbers of angels, 1+1+3+2+ . . . : nineteen. That was it, a code and a key.

Bylot rearranged the numbers in his head to fit with the keys he had used in Dee's workshop: $_1 1_3 2_2 2_1 1_1 1_2 1_1$. Skip the first letter, take 1, skip the next 3, take 2. Feverishly, Bylot translated. Apollo rest only alone—portolan! The portolan lay backward within the earthly sphere! Even Uriel's prophecy at the skrying had told him that—the earthly sphere contained the answer to his dreams. Now he knew why the smallest level of the alchemist's globe, the earthly sphere, had always seemed vaguely familiar.

Dropping Trithemius to the floor, Bylot hauled himself back out of his chair and went to the mantle. He picked up the alchemist's globe and peered deep within. Even with the aid of his spectacles, he could not make out the details, but he knew what to do. Replacing the globe, he carefully removed one of the magnifying lenses from his spectacles. Holding it in front of the other, Bylot adjusted the distances until the inner sphere leaped into magnified clarity.

For an age, Bylot was motionless. Eventually, his breath clouded the lens and he drew back with a sigh. It was difficult to see clearly through the swirling liquids and against the elements within, but there could be no doubt. The engravings were a map—minute and carved in a mirror image of a true globe. Everything was there in exquisite detail, Africa, Europe, Asia, the Americas and the undiscovered *Terra Australis*. Through Bylot's primitive telescope they were recognizable. More complete than on any map Bylot had ever seen. There was no more *terra incognita*.

Bylot rotated the globe until the northernmost part of the Americas lay beneath his magnified gaze. There was Greenland, no bigger than a flea, Davis's Strait and Baffin's Bay. The Furious Overfall was there, too, no broader than a hair's width and leading into the Great Sea that Bylot knew so well. Yet this globe had been etched long before Hudson and Bylot had sailed there. All the wondrous geographic knowledge of the ancients was here, recorded who knew how far back in the mists of time and hidden in plain view from all but the most astute observer. It was a true portolan, a complete map of the world, the answer to Bylot's dream.

With a shaking hand, Bylot replaced his eyeglass lens in its frame and returned to his chair. He laughed—a harsh, ironic laugh. Another what if. If only he hadn't been so self-absorbed that winter of 1611–12. If only he had understood Dee's inscription then. He would have seen the portolan and known that the Great Sea was but a bay, Drake's entrance to the Straits of Anian but a false temptation, and the distance between the two an impossibility. Had he known that, he might have sailed south on a rescue mission. But the other question remained unanswered—would any have lived to be rescued? When he answered that question, too, he would be able to rest.

Bending forward, Bylot picked up Hudson's journal from the table and, with a deep sigh, tugged at the clasp that held the book closed. It refused to open and his skinny, arthritic fingers were not strong enough to force it. Bylot cursed in frustration.

At that instant, a loud knocking on the street door made Bylot jump. He glanced at his window. It was still fully dark outside, but the noises on the High Street had died away to a few isolated shouts and curses.

The knocking was repeated, louder this time.

"Leave me alone," Bylot grumbled. "I wish no more intercourse with the world. My world is here in this book and in my memory."

The knocking persisted.

"Go! Leave me!" Bylot shouted.

A voice from the street replied. "Master Bylot. It is Robert Gilby. I have something else of interest to you."

"I have the book and you have the money. What else could interest me?"

"Ah, but Master Bylot, the book was not all I saved from the ancient savage. But I am sure you are as disinclined as I to conduct business on the street at this ungodly hour. Let me in and we can talk of terms like civilized men."

Bylot hesitated. What else could Gilby have? The portolan that Staffe had saved? That was worth nothing to him now . . . but perhaps it was some other written record?

"Why did you not tell me of this last time?"

"My motive was simply profit. I thought to draw you in with the book and I see, since you are not yet abed, that I have done so. I wish, like any good man of business, to increase my profit to the fullest. Yet I shall not see you wronged. I seek only fair recompense for my labour. Let me in and we can discuss terms."

Bylot doubted that "fair" was a word Gilby ever used honestly. Nonetheless, the story made sense and gold sovereigns were of no use now. At the very least, Gilby would be able to open the journal's clasp.

"I shall come down."

Slowly, Bylot replaced the book, picked up a candle from the table and descended the stairs. He held the candle in his left hand and felt along the wall with his right. Each step ached and he was frighteningly aware that his old bones could hardly bear his weight as his feet searched for each succeeding step.

"Come on, old man," Gilby shouted through the door. "It is cold as the grave out here."

"You do not have the patience of a man of business," Bylot replied.

At last he reached the door and pulled the bolt. He had barely begun to swing it inward when a heavy weight was thrown violently against the outside. The door crashed wide, catching Bylot a hard blow to the temple and hurling him painfully back onto the stairs. His left hand, holding the candle twisted under him as he fell and Bylot heard a loud crack as he landed. The candle extinguished and Bylot vaguely saw two shadows pushing past him in the darkness before he blacked out.

Ψ

Bylot's first awareness was of the contrast between the warm blood coursing down his cheek and the cold of his skin from the wind coming in the open door. He touched his head with his right hand and winced as he found the gash on his left temple. The wooden stairs dug into his back. Bylot tried to push himself up and gasped as pain shot down his left arm. He remembered the crack as he fell.

Bylot cursed softly. He was angry at himself for having trusted Gilby. The man, and an accomplice, had merely come back to rob him. Bylot laughed bitterly, his desire to know had seduced him into opening the door to Gilby a second time. Now he would die without ever knowing the answer.

"No!" Bylot croaked out the denial. He would die, but he would know the answer first. Gilby had been after gold, perhaps he had ignored or missed the journal. Perhaps Bylot's salvation was still by his chair.

Pulling on the door handle with his good arm, Bylot slowly hauled himself to his feet. His left arm hung uselessly by his side. Touching gingerly, he discovered a bump beneath the skin of his mid-forearm where there should have been only smooth bone. The bump was tender, but there was surprisingly little pain.

Holding his broken arm against his body, Bylot used his good shoulder to close the door. He leaned heavily against it until the dizziness passed. He heard a loud crash from upstairs. They were still here!

Brushing against the right-hand wall so he didn't bump his arm, Bylot slowly climbed the stairs. He had no wish to confront the ransackers, but he had to make sure the journal was safe. That was all he wished for—that and enough remaining life to read it. The rest was vanity and Gilby could have it all. Much good might it do him. All Bylot's gold would be worth but a few drinks and a few hours with a low woman, if it didn't earn him a blade between the ribs from his cutpurse companion. Bylot struggled upward.

The dull light of the fire illuminated a scene of devastation. Books and manuscripts were strewn about, many ripped open and scattered. His shelves had been cleared and their contents lay on the floor, shattered if they were too fragile to withstand the fall. His chair lay on its side, its insides laid open through numerous gaping slashes. A man he didn't recognize was busy adding to the destruction, violently emptying the book chest in the corner. Only the mantle above the dying fire was undisturbed.

Bylot sighed with relief as he saw Henry Hudson's journal lying unnoticed beside the hearth. Unsteadily, he stepped into the room. The man paused in his search and looked at him unsure what to do.

At that moment, a victorious shout came from the next room, "I have it!"

Gilby appeared, clutching a bag that Bylot knew contained every farthing that remained to him.

"I have found the old miser's hoard," Gilby yelled triumphantly. Then he noticed Bylot. "So we have not killed you yet, old man."

"Nor shall you," Bylot replied as defiantly as he could. "I have not come this far in the world to have my life ended by the likes of you, Robert Gilby. I have known many men in my years, some good, some evil, some who presumed to know the cosmos as gods and some who were happy to find contentment in the simple beauty of the natural world. You are not worthy to clean the boots of the least of them. Take your ill-gotten wealth and choke long and hard upon what it buys you."

Bylot struggled to keep his focus on Gilby. If he could keep the man's anger directed at him, he might ignore the book and leave him to his task.

Gilby took a step forward, his faced masked in anger.

"Come, Robert," his companion said. "We have the money. Let us go enjoy it."

Gilby's face broke into a wicked smile. "Aye, we shall do that. But I do not wish to leave a witness. Count this." Gilby tossed the heavy sack to his accomplice and took a step toward Bylot. A thin blade appeared in his hand. "I shall attend to business."

Bylot shrank back. He considered making a break for the street door, but should he, by some miracle, manage to beat the young, fit Gilby to it, what good would it do? Even if there were someone outside, none at this hour would interfere in just another street fight. Too many people died in the filth of back alleys to warrant much attention.

And it would mean leaving the journal. Hudson's words were all Bylot had to live for, so, if he were to die it should at least be in an attempt to save them. Bylot stumbled awkwardly toward the hearth.

At the same moment, Gilby lunged, but not at Bylot. Gilby leaped at his companion who stood bemused, holding the sack of money. Before the man could react, Gilby's arm came up, and the blade slid beneath his ribs and up to tear open his heart.

The force of the blow lifted the man off his feet and knocked the bag from his grasp, spilling sovereigns, crowns and guineas across the floor in a glittering flood. As he landed, Gilby withdrew the knife and plunged it into the man's throat. He had time only to register a surprised gasp before bright blood welled out of his mouth and he collapsed beside the money. Blood, black in the firelight, ran from his wounds and seeped between the gold coins. The body jerked once and the man's eyes rolled back. It was over in seconds.

Bylot was standing by the ruins of his chair, the journal at his feet. His eyes skittered from the dead man to Gilby, who stood smiling back at him.

"I am sorry my companion ruined your chair, but you have no need of such luxury now."

Gilby wiped the blade of his knife on his sleeve and stepped forward. Bylot stepped back. His left elbow bumped the fireplace, causing him to jerk in pain. To prevent himself falling, he thrust his right hand out and grasped the edge of the mantle. Bylot felt a cold sweat bead on his face and he had to take several deep breaths to bring the room back into focus.

Gilby's smiled broadened into a laugh. "You old fool. I doubt I shall be hastening God's work by much. What can you have to live for anyway? You sit here alone while the real world is out there to be taken by the neck and enjoyed. And that is what I intend to do. There is enough gold here to finance my simple pleasures for some time. You cannot defend it, so I shall take it."

"But I give it to you. Why must you kill?" Bylot felt the roundness of the alchemist's globe against his fingers.

Gilby shrugged. "I do not like loose ends. If I do not kill you, who knows what friends you may have who might feel a foolish desire to see you revenged."

"I have no friends."

"I think you are telling the truth and, in any case, I doubt you will live long enough to talk to them, but I do not like risk. This shall be cleaner."

Bylot glanced down at the journal. He hadn't meant to, but he couldn't help himself. Gilby followed the look. "So you haven't even read it yet." He hooked a toe under the volume. "Much good it would do you, in any case." The toe flipped up, flinging the book toward Bylot. The clasp cracked against the side of the stone hearth, breaking from the rotting covers. Ragged pages fanned in the flickering light as it fell into the fire.

"No!" Without stopping to think, Bylot grasped the globe and hurled it at Gilby with all the force left in his body. His left arm swung against the fireplace and he lost his balance, sliding awkwardly to the hearth, jaw clenched against the waves of pain flowing up his arm.

The globe struck Gilby a hard blow on the left cheek, shattering the fragile glass and mixing the contents into a violently unstable soup. All the powers of the alchemist's world exploded in a searing flash that, for an instant, illuminated the room as brightly as the noonday sun. As an unearthly scream echoed from Gilby, Bylot remembered Dee's warnings about the power of the globe.

By the time Bylot's eyes recovered from the glare, Gilby's face was surrounded by a halo of flame. A hot, corrosive liquid was eating into his eyes and skin.

Gilby's knife lay now on the floor beside him and his hands were raised, tearing at the agony of his melting face. His hands scrabbled uselessly at the blistering flesh, serving only to transfer the pain to his fingers and palms.

Waving his arms insanely, Gilby stumbled around the devastated room, spreading bloody coins about him in his panic. His screams had become gurgling gasps as the liquid, drawn deep into his chest by his frantic breathing, destroyed his throat and began eating into his lungs.

Bylot felt his eyes sting and his throat catch with the fumes. In fascinated horror, he watched as the thing that used to be a man stumbled to a stop and sank to its knees. Slowly, Gilby turned what was left of his face toward Bylot. He was no longer recognizable. His eyes were black, hollow sockets and most of his lips were gone, revealing a hideous parody of a smile. Strips of flesh hung from his cheeks and hands, and his arms twitched uncontrollably. The teeth opened as if the thing were trying to speak, but all that emerged was a series of hiccups before Gilby pitched forward onto the floor.

The rattle of the head landing on the pile of money broke the spell. Ignoring the pain, Bylot turned to the fire and frantically scooped Hudson's journal out of the flames. Using his right sleeve, he beat out the fires that had established a grip on the book. As the last of them was reduced to a wisp of smoke, Bylot sagged back against the fireplace, cradling his broken forearm on his lap.

As his breathing returned to something like normal, Bylot dragged the book to him. The edges of the pages were blackened and the cover was burned through in places, but the heavy wooden boards had protected most of the precious document.

Bylot was exhausted. His left arm throbbed and blood dripped from his head wound onto his chest. His right hand was blackened and blistering where he had thrust it into the hot coals to rescue the book. But none of that would kill him just yet. Gilby had failed. With a little bit of luck, Bylot would live long enough to read the story.

With a smile on his face, Robert Bylot opened the book and stared in horror at the unreadable first page. He turned to the next—it was the same. In an increasing frenzy and ignoring the agony of his burned hand, Bylot tore through the remaining pages. It was no use. What had once been fine script was smeared and smudged. Some pages were torn in half and dark stains obscured others. Others were so rotted that they crumbled under Bylot's touch. Occasionally a word was legible, but these were as meaningless as the unconnected utterings of Gilby's savage. Time, water and decay had taken Hudson's words—and Bylot's answer—to a place he could never reach.

Bylot sighed. Then he laughed. There was no resolution. His hopes for a clear ending had simply been another arrogance. Even the portolan on the alchemist's globe was now lost. Bylot sagged back against the stone fireplace, his broken arm lying uselessly on his knee. The burned fingers of his right hand lay curled, like a large dead spider, amid the ruined pages of the book.

Bylot was almost unnaturally aware of everything around him, the soft sigh of a burned-through log collapsing in the grate, the way the weak firelight sparkled off the broken glass on the floor, the throat-catching fumes from the alchemist's globe hanging in the air, the harsh edges of the broken chair and the barely recognizable features on the face of the body behind it. This was the present, a crystal fragment of his life as painfully sharp as the sun through a spyglass, made more real because it was one of his last.

There were no answers. It was all bones and dust now. Nothing bound the story together, not Dee's dreams of empire, the fabled northwest passage or the mysterious portolan—they all meant nothing. Bylot would never know. It was all a petty human drama, meaningless in the vast melting pot of time. But still Bylot wondered, did any live? Could he have saved Hudson and the others the summer following the mutiny?

Bylot stared at Hudson's journal as if, by an effort of will alone, he could force the pages to give up their secrets. He smiled ruefully and moved his body to ease the pain in his arm. As he did so, the book slid from his lap. A folded sheet fell out from beneath the back board.

Bylot picked it up and carefully unfolded the brittle paper. It was a fragment of a hand-drawn map. It was stained and faint, but the lines were discernible. They showed the Furious Overfall, Michaelmass Bay, the Great Sea that was now coming to be known as Hudson Bay. It showed the western shore, unbroken by a passage, as Bylot had discovered on Button's voyage in 1612. This was a piece of the map that Staffe had saved—the map that Bylot had seen on Hudson's desk before the mutiny; the portolan that Greene had taken to the great cabin and which had finally destroyed Henry Hudson's dreams. This was why Hudson's resolve was already destroyed before the mutiny even broke out.

Bylot turned the paper over. There was writing on the back and, unlike the journal pages, it was faint but readable— a few paragraphs in an unfamiliar hand.

Bylot caught the first words, "My father was the last to die."

The final question was answered after all.

*My father was the last to die.*

*Wydehouse was the first. I think he expired in the rough handling when we were cast adrift. Fanner and Moore did not long survive him, and all three were cast into the waters of the bay. After the Discovery sailed from view, Staffe was in favour of continuing the chase, but Ludlowe and Butte argued for making land in order to find sustenance. This we did.*

*Staffe and Butte took the musket and a spear and went hunting. They never returned. Whether they were overcome by wild beasts or simply lost their way, I know not. Ludlowe lost heart, refusing even to eat the small fish I managed to catch. He wasted to death despite my pleas.*

*My father and I lived alone for the summer, surviving on berries, fish and the occasional small animals I could trap. As the weather turned cold we burned what we could to keep warm—the shallop, Staffe's tools and chest, and the charts he had saved. The only thing I refused to burn was this journal. Then the savages found us.*

*My father died that winter of a fever, talking to my mother and brother as if they were by his side. I laid his body out after the fashion of the savages and waited.*

*It has been five years now and none have come for me. I have learned some of the savage tongue and ask all whom we meet for word of strange canoes, but there is nothing.*

*I do not mind now. It is not a bad life. The land supplies all needs and there is an attraction to living simply without dreams. I think it is time to stop waiting. My new family know of a woman who would make me a good wife, so I think I shall marry and take what life here can offer. I even have a savage name, as close as they can come to my real name in their tongue—Dja-khu-tsan.*

*I shall preserve this book as best I can against the day that others of my kind may come to this land. Perhaps it will explain what happened to us. Still and all, I cannot help asking myself—did any live?*

*Jack Hudson*

It was odd, Bylot thought. In a short while, the only survivor of his story would be an ancient savage sitting by a fire in the wilderness. Perhaps it was fitting that everything—Dee's mysticism, Smythe's greed, Greene's games—should come to this. It was all just dust now and who could say that the life Dja-khu-tsan found amongst the savages was not more fulfilling and satisfying than what would have been his lot had he returned to London? Perhaps the simplest things were the best. After all, a few moments of warmth before a fire was of greater value now to Bylot than all the schemes of Aristotle or Copernicus.

Slowly, Bylot lifted the useless book in his burned right hand. Holding it by its blackened spine, he let the pages fan open between the covers, then, grunting with the pain, he launched it onto the glowing embers of the fire.

Orange flames jumped from the coals to the dry pages. They rustled between the lost words, voraciously consuming the past and turning it into flakes of ash that swirled and raced each other up the chimney into tomorrow's dawn. With a final effort, Bylot placed the map fragment and Jack Hudson's last note on top. He watched as the edges curled and blackened.

Bylot leaned back, enjoying the final warmth from the burning book. The flakes of ash carried his guilt with them. It had been a long, hard night but the story was complete. His ghosts had been laid to rest and now he, too, could find peace.

The book boards in the fire, eaten through by the flames, collapsed in a tiny explosion of sparks and fragments of blackened paper. Starved, the flames died, leaving only glowing coals. Bylot felt fingers of the chill dawn clutch at him.

Bylot looked up. Evelyn stood serene amidst the wreckage of the room. She was dressed as Bylot remembered her from the day he had returned to Hoddesdon. "Come," she said as she held out her hand. "There is still much to learn."

Bylot smiled. All the prophecies had come true: he had become an explorer but his discoveries had been credited to others; he had been happy during those two short years in London with Evelyn and he was happy again now that he had seen the world as it truly was on the earthly sphere of the alchemist's globe.

"I'm coming, Evelyn," Bylot said. He sighed and closed his eyes. Contentedly, he embraced the final alchemy.

# Historical Note

A lot of *The Alchemist's Dream*, including much of the stranger stuff, is real. Every main character, with the sole exception of Evelyn, is in the historical record, although I have had to give them personalities from my imagination.

Henry Greene is a composite based on John Dee's real skryer, Edward Kelley, and a mysterious passenger that Henry Hudson brought on board in the Thames Estuary. No one has ever satisfactorily explained Greene's role on the voyage or in the mutiny, or why Hudson brought such an obvious landsman aboard.

Henry Hudson's wife, Katherine, was indeed a strong-willed woman. After Hudson was lost, she badgered Smythe to pay her compensation, which she used to voyage to India where she made a fortune trading. She returned to London a rich woman. The fictional Evelyn might have grown into a woman like Katherine, had she lived.

Hudson's oldest son, Richard, moved to North America where he prospered and where his descendants still live.

Robert Bylot is one of the great mysteries of exploration. He was obviously a very accomplished navigator, although nothing is known of how he learned his trade. He appears as a member of the crew on Henry Hudson's fourth and final voyage, was made the ship's mate, survived the mutiny and brought the *Discovery* home. Bylot did go back the following year with Captain Button and was pilot on both of William Baffin's voyages. He was probably never given a ship of his own because his name was tainted with mutiny. Had he been given a ship, Baffin Bay and Baffin Island might well be Bylot Bay and Island today. Nothing is known of Bylot's life after Baffin's second voyage—he disappears as mysteriously as he appeared.

I have stayed close to the historical record—for example, some of the dialogue during the mutiny is taken from Abacuk Prickett's account—but two changes require mention. Most obviously, the book is not written in Elizabethan English. If it were, it would be almost unreadable today, so I have modernized the dialogue, although I have tried to retain a flavour of the speech of the time.

The second change is in keeping Henry Greene alive after the *Discovery* returned. According to Prickett, he died with Wilson, Perce and Thomas in the attack at Digges Island. Of course, Prickett is not the most reliable witness, and it is very suspicious that all the leaders of the mutiny died on the voyage back.

The surviving mutineers were eventually tried in 1618 and acquitted. Why none were punished in the days when mutiny was a virtual death sentence if caught is also unexplained. The idea that they were too valuable to kill is probably close to the truth.

John Dee was one of the most powerful men of his time and was favoured by Queen Elizabeth. He advised on many of the major English voyages of discovery in the late sixteenth century and is considered by some to be the father of modern chemistry. He also searched for the Philosopher's Stone, communed with angels through skryers and crystals, and believed in the Golden Age of Troy. He was a man of his time, with one foot in the modern world and the other in the mysticism of the Middle Ages.

Finally, did the portolan of the world exist? Probably not, although many people at the time believed that there were ancient maps and accounts of long-dead sailors that contained forgotten information and wisdom. Columbus, on his voyage of 1492, apparently had a map with him that he consulted on several occasions. Perhaps he knew more of where he was going than we give him credit for.

If such maps existed, they would have been kept secret as much too valuable to allow into competitors' hands. It was a secretive age, and no one kept secrets better than Queen Elizabeth and her network of spies. In 1579, Francis Drake probably did sail much farther north than was publicly admitted after he returned to England, and he may well have discovered what he thought was the eastern entrance to the Straits of Anian close to 58 degrees. His Nova Albion might be Vancouver Island. For a time, when Davis, Hudson and Bylot were exploring, it was believed that the Northwest Passage was short and easily attainable. It was not, and Henry Hudson wasn't the only one to die looking for it.

As Robert Bylot proved, the true Northwest Passage is not out of Hudson Bay. It is the one far to the north on Dee's map, and no one passed that way for another 300 years.

# Acknowledgements

What little we know for certain of Henry Hudson's voyages is collected masterfully in Donald S. Johnson's *Charting the Sea of Darkness*. He provided the solid base from which my imagination deviated. *Nathaniel's Nutmeg* by Giles Milton tells a wonderful story and gives a vivid sense of the struggle the voyagers went through to secure a hold full of spices in the early seventeenth century, and Benjamin Woolley's *The Queen's Conjurer* brings the strange ideas and the world of John Dee to life. Although he was talking about a different year, Daniel Defoe's *A Journal of the Plague Year* contributed greatly to the poignancy of Evelyn's tragedy.

A wide variety of websites supplied fascinating details on maps and the universe Robert Bylot inhabited, but an excellent starting point is http://www.ianchadwick.com/hudson/.

As he did with *Where Soldiers Lie*, Luc Normandin has provided the text with a stunning visual reality, and without Linda Pruessen's magical editorial alchemy that text would not be half what it is.

As always, Jenifer has accepted with understanding that part of my life is lived in the distant past.

My thanks to all.